AAKHIRI KHAT

DIVYANI GUPTA

Made with ♥ on the Notion Press Platform
www.notionpress.com

To every soul carrying an unfinished story, and to every letter that never found its destination.

Contents

Contents

CHAPTER ONE

The Last Page

The room was silent except for the scratching of pen and paper.

Rishikesh adjusted his spectacles and looked at the unfinished manuscript lying on his desk. The table lamp cast a warm circle of light over hundreds of handwritten pages.

Another page.

Rishikesh crumpled it and threw it towards the overflowing dustbin.

Missed.

The paper rolled across the floor and came to the near dozen of its fallen companions.

He leaned back in his chair and rubbed his eyes. The fresh page on his desk seemed to mock him.

Forty four years old. Eight bestselling books. Thousand of pages written.

Yet a single page refused to be completed.

The last page.

The one that mattered the most.

He picked up his pen and tried again.

A few words.

A sentence.

Then he stopped.

"No" he muttered.

The sheet met the same fate as the others.

A soft knock on the door broke the silence .

Before he could answer, the door opened.

"Dad?"

Kehkasha stepped inside carrying two cups of tea. Her eyes immediately travelled to the battlefield of crumpled papers scatteres around the room.

She raised an eyebrow.

"Should I be worried?"

Rishikesh smiled faintly.

"You should be worried about the amount of paper I have murdered today"

She laughed and placed a cup beside him.

"The last page again?"

He nodded.

"I've written this story a hundred times in my head, Kehkasha. But when I try to finish it..." His voice trailed off. "The words refuse to come."

She glanced at the manuscript lying on the desk.

The title staring back at her.

Akhiri Khat

For a moment, neither of them spoke. Then kehkasha pulled a chair and sat beside him.

"Maybe you're forcing it." Rishikesh looked at her. "Maybe today isn't the day it ends."

"And when will that day come?"

"When *Destiny* decides" She smiles.

He chukled. "Thats a very convenient answer"

"No" she said softly. "I mean it. Some letters are not written by people, dad. They are written by destiny. They reach where they are meant to reach, and they stop where they're meant to stop"

For a moment, Rishikesh simply looked at her. His little daughter had grown so wise.

He closed the manuscript.

"Come on." Kehkasha frowned.

"What? You brought tea?"

"Yes, and now we're drinking it before it gets cold."

The smile returned to her face. Together, they left the room. The unfinished manuscript remained on the desk. The last page was still blank waiting for its final letter.

CHAPTER TWO

THE POET NOBODY KNEW

Twenty Five Years Earlier...

Year 2003

Rishikesh had become a name every student in the college knew within just a few months of his admission. A first-year student pursuing Bachelor's in Finance, he was impossible to ignore. Some knew him as the boy who could break noses in fights without blinking, some admired him as the all-rounder who excelled in almost everything he touched. Whether it was athletics, debating, or dancing at the annual functions, Rishikesh somehow managed to stand out effortlessly.

He was tall, broad-shouldered, and carried a personality that kept most people from messing with him. Seniors disliked his arrogance, juniors admired his fearlessness, and professors often sighed at the trouble he attracted despite being exceptionally talented.

But those who truly knew him, knew another side as well. A fiercely loyal, soft hearted friend. A boy who pretended not to care, yet quietly paid for his classmates' tea when they ran out of money, and perhaps most importantly, a boy who laughed at the idea of love, the idea of destiny and the idea of god.

That afternoon, Rishikesh sat lazily on the basketball court boundary while Varun munched peanuts beside him.

"You know what your problem is?" Varun said, throwing a peanut at him.

Rishikesh rolled his eyes. "Here we go again."

"You think you're invincible. One day a girl will come and fix this attitude of yours."

Rishikesh burst out laughing. "Me? In love? I'd rather fail my finals."

Varun grinned. "Mark my words. The same guy who breaks bones will one day be mad for a girl."

"Disgusting," Rishikesh replied dramatically. "Love is mankind's biggest scam."

Varun shook his head, smiling at his friend's confidence, unaware that destiny was already laughing somewhere and pulls out his blue Nokia 1100 to play the classic snake game until the bell rings for next lecture.

A week later, the college annual fest was in full swing. The auditorium was packed with students cheering, singing and shouting. Rishikesh had participated in the dance competition earlier and was now waiting impatiently for the event to end.

On the stage, a student was reciting a poem. The entire auditorium fell silent.

Rishikesh frowned, he never cared for poetry. But he kept listening. Every line seemed to carry a strange weight, as if someone had poured pieces of their soul onto paper. The hall fell silent as the verse ended. For a moment, nobody moved. Then the applause began again. Louder this time. Rishikesh joined it absent mindedly.

Varun looked at him suspiciously. "Since when did you start liking poetry?"

Rishikesh didn't take his eyes off the stage. A small smile appeared on his face.

"Since now."

Varun widened his eyes. "Oh God."

A few minutes later, the host returned to the stage. "The poem was written by one of our first-year students from the Literature Department."

Rishikesh sat up slightly.

"Aashna"

The name appeared on the screen behind the stage. Aashna. No surname, No photograph, Just a name. For reasons he couldn't explain he repeated it silently. Aashna..

The program continued , but his attention had already drifted elsewhere. As the event ended, students poured out the auditorium. Rishikesh found himself scanning faces.

"Looking for someone?" Varun asked.

"The poet."

"The poet?"

"The girl who wrote that poem"

Varun laughed. "You don't even know what she looks like."

"I Know."

"Then how are you planning to find her?"

Rishikesh had no answer.

Still, his eyes continued searching. Within minutes, the crowd had dispersed. The mystery remained. The only thing he had was a name.

Aashna.

CHAPTER THREE

THE FIRST LETTER

The college library was unusually quiet that afternoon. Rows of books stood like silent spectators as Rishikesh wandered between the shelves, searching for something worth reading for his creative assement coming next week.He had already rejected three novels.

One was too predictable. One was too boring. And the third had a cover so dramatic that he refused to trust it.His fingers stopped on a worn paperback tucked between two thick volumes."Maybe you'll be different," he murmured, pulling it out.As he opened the first page, something slipped out and landed on the floor. A yellow sticky note. Curious, he picked it up. The handwriting was neat, slightly slanted.

"Not worth reading, read 'The Namesake' instead..

Aashna:)"

A smile escaped him, Aashna, the girl behind that poem. Who leaves reviews inside library books? He looked around. The library appeared exactly as it always did. Silent. Ordinary. Yet somehow, it suddenly felt less ordinary.

A few minutes later, he found a copy of The Namesake. When he opened it, another sticky note fell into his hands. This time he laughed.

"Hey fellow reader..

If you finish this book, leave your thoughts in the last cupboard near the corner window.

- Aashna:)"

For a moment, Rishikesh simply stared at the note. Then he tucked it carefully into his pocket. Challenge accepted.

That night, he read until dawn. The story kept him emotionally invested. And the moment the library opened the next morning, he was standing outside. Feeling slightly ridiculous, he took out a sticky note and wrote:

"Hey Aashna!"

The book was beautiful. Emotional enough to keep me awake the entire night. Thanks for the recommendation. And by the way, I heaard your poem at the college fest last week. It would've been even excellent if you recited it yourself.

-Rishikesh"

He folded the note and placed it on the last shelf of the corner cupboard. Then he walked away before he could change his mind.

The next day, he returned. There was a new note waiting. His heart betrayed him by beating a little faster.

"Thankyou, dear rishikesh!

I'm glad you liked the book. And about the poem...I prefer staying backstage. I want people to notice my work, not me.

-Aashna:)"

He read the note twice. Then a third time.

The following morning, another sticky note appeared on the shelf. This time, beside it lay two small sunflowers. The note read:

"Maybe most people notice only your work. but this fellow listener noticed you too.

-Rishikesh"

CHAPTER FOUR

INK AND CONVERSATIONS

"You've changed." Varun's voice echoed across the canteen.

Rishikesh didn't bother looking up. "You said that five minutes ago."

"And I'll keep saying it until you explain what happened to you." Varun snatched the sticky note from his hand.

Rishikesh immediately stood up. "Give it back."

Varun stared at the note dramatically. "Wow."

He looked up. "The guy who once got suspended for punching three seniors now spends his mornings reading colourful sticky notes."

Rishikesh rolled his eyes. "Are you done?"

"No." Varun folded his arms. "Who is Aashna?"

Rishikesh nearly choked on his tea. "Nobody."

"Ah yes. Nobody." Varun pointed towards the note. "People usually don't smile at notes written by nobody."

Rishikesh grabbed the paper back. "Mind your business."

Varun laughed. "My business is exactly this."

Rishikesh regretted telling him about the library cupboard. At that time, it had seemed harmless. Now he had become the source of Varun's daily entertainment. The rest of the day passed in lectures. But between every class, Rishikesh found himself thinking about a girl he had never met. A girl whose face he didn't know. A girl who somehow felt familiar.

The next morning, he reached the library before his first lecture. The cupboard waited silently. A new note rested on the shelf. His lips curved automatically.

"Good morning fellow reader!

Did you know people often judge a book by its cover, yet rarely take the time to read what's inside?

-Aashna"

He laughed. Then sat down nearby and began writing.

"Good morning!

Did you know some people hide between the pages so well that others are left searching for them chapter after chapter? By the way I still think you should've recited your poem yourself at the fest.

-Rishikesh"

The reply arrived the following day.

"And I still think poems should be remembered, not the poets.

-Aashna"

The conversation continued. Day after day. Book recommendations became discussions. Discussions became debates. Debates became stories. He learned that she loved rain, as much as he hated it. She told him she collected old letters. He admitted he had never written one before meeting her. Slowly, the notes grew longer. And so did the wait between them.

One evening, after staring at an empty sticky note for ten minutes, Rishikesh finally gathered enough courage.

"Okay, important question. Will I ever know your name?"

He stared at the note. Then folded it. Then unfolded it. Then folded it again. Eventually, he left it in the cupboard. The next day, he arrived at the library with an excitement he refused to acknowledge. There was already a reply waiting.

"You alrady do, It's written at the end of every note.

-Aashna"

Rishikesh laughed despite himself. The next note he left read:

"I meant the real you,

The girl behind the name, the girl behind these notes.

I want to know you.

-Rishikesh"

The next morning, his heart pounded harder than it should have while opening the cupboard. Aashna teased him with a single note saying

"Zara ruko janaab kya iraada? hai kyun kareeb aa rahe ho?

Dekho tum khud aag ki taraf kadam bada rahe ho..

Agar ye ishq hai to rok lo khudko

kyu khamakha ek patthar se dil laga rahe ho..

-Aashna"

Somehow the note made Rishikesh blush, he laughed to himself and invested almost a day to frame a comparative reply

"Ab bada chuka hoon kadam lautna mera eimaan nahin,

Kehti ho khud ko shama to mai parwana ban ke jal jaaunga..

Bada guroor hai tumhe apni berukhi par to dekhna,

Mere ishq ki taakat se is patthar me jaan launga..

-Rishikesh"

The next note followed with

"Damn you never told me that you write.. the wordings are wonderful!

-Aashna"

Rishikesh leaves another note saying

"Wonderful enough to convince you to meet? Miss Aashna..

-Rishikesh"

"Come on! If we're destined to meet, we'll meet. Let's leave it to ***destiny****.*

-Aashna"

Rishikesh read the note once. Then twice. Then a third time.

Destiny.

For some reason, the word stayed with him long after he left the library. That night, before sleeping, he placed every sticky note she had ever written inside a small box. Then he picked up the latest one. For a long moment, he stared at the word.

Destiny.

A strange smile appeared on his face. He didn't know anything about her life. He didn't know her face. He didn't know her voice. Yet somehow, he was already hoping destiny would agree.

CHAPTER FIVE

The Testimony of Destiny

By the time Rishikesh stepped out of the examination hall, it looked as though the sky had declared war on the city. He stared at the downpour. Then at the question paper in his hand. Then back at the rain. "I genuinely don't know which one was worse," he muttered. Varun laughed.

"The exam."

"The rain."

"The exam."

"The rain."

"The exam."

Rishikesh sighed. "Fine. The exam."

The two friends hurried beneath the nearest shade. Students rushed in every direction, some laughing, some complaining, some already discussing answers that Rishikesh wanted to forget existed.

"Tea?" Varun suggested. Rishikesh nodded immediately. Some tragedies required tea. The roadside stall near the college was crowded as usual. Steam rose from boiling kettles while the smell of ginger and cardamom filled the air. For a few minutes, neither of them spoke.

Rishikesh stood watching the rain.

Then something caught his eye.

Across the road, near a small tree, a girl crouched beneath an umbrella. No. Not beneath it. The umbrella lay forgotten beside her. The rain had soaked the sleeves of her purple kurti. Hair all wet, a few stubborn strands had escaped and kept falling across her cheek. Yet she seemed completely unconcerned. She was smiling. A smile so genuine that it made the gloomy afternoon seem brighter. Three tiny puppies had gathered around her. She tore pieces from a packet of biscuits and fed them one by one. The puppies wagged their tails furiously. The girl laughed.

And for a brief moment, the entire world seemed to pause.

Rishikesh couldn't explain it. Something about her felt familiar. His eyes remained fixed on her. His heart had begun behaving strangely Faster. Louder. As if it knew something he didn't.

Then she looked up. Straight in his curious, brown eyes; they were too honest for this world

For a moment, the rest of the world faded into the background. The rain, The traffic, The voices from the tea stall. Everything disappeared.

Her eyes were the first thing he noticed. Deep and expressive. The kind of eyes that looked as though they carried entire stories within them. He forgot what he had been thinking. Forgot about the disastrous exam, forgot about everthing except the girl standing a few steps away

The feeling intensified.

A ridiculous thought crossed his mind.

Impossible.

Yet it refused to leave.

What if...What if it was her? His fingers tightened around the paper cup.

Months of conversations. Months of notes. Months of wondering.

Without realizing it, he took a step forward. Then another. The rain instantly soaked his shirt. Varun shouted something behind him. He didn't hear a word. The girl was still looking at him.

Confused now. Curious. His throat suddenly felt dry.

This was absurd. What if he was wrong? What if she wasn't Aashna? What if he embarrassed himself in front of a complete stranger? The sensible thing would have been to walk away. Instead, he heard himself say—

"Aashna?"

The girl froze.

The puppies continued eating. The rain continued falling. For a second, neither of them moved. Then her eyebrows lifted.

"Wait." She stood up. "Do you know me?"

Rishikesh laughed nervously.

Months of preparation vanished from his mind. All the clever things he had imagined saying disappeared. Only the truth remained.

"I'm Rishikesh." Silence. The world suddenly felt very quiet despite the rain.

Aashna stared at him.

He stared back.

There she was. The girl behind the poems. The handwriting. The notes. The cupboard. The sunflowers.

Real. Standing right in front of him.

Neither knew what to say. Neither wanted to ruin the moment.

Finally, Aashna smiled. The same smile he had imagined countless times without ever knowing its shape. And somehow, it was better. Much better.

"You look different," she said.

Rishikesh blinked. "You've never seen me."

"I know." Her smile widened. "But somehow I expected something else."

He laughed. "Good different or bad different?"

"Still deciding."

For the first time in weeks, he felt completely relaxed. Then suddenly remembered something.

"Tea."

"What?"

"Would you like some tea?"

Aashna nodded.

A few minutes later they stood beneath the stall's roof, holding steaming cups. The conversation flowed surprisingly easily. As if they weren't strangers meeting for the first time. As if they were simply continuing a conversation paused the previous day. They talked about books. Poetry. The exam. The puppies. The rain. Mostly the rain.

Then disaster struck.

While trying to gesture dramatically during a story, Rishikesh accidentally knocked his own cup. The tea lurched forward. Straight toward Aashna's hand. Without thinking, he grabbed her wrist and pulled it away. The hot tea splashed across his own fingers instead.

"Ouch!"

Aashna burst out laughing.

Rishikesh stared at his reddened hand. Then at her. Then began laughing too.

"What an impressive first meeting."

"Very memorable," she agreed.

"Please pretend that didn't happen."

"Absolutely not."

They continued laughing.

For the first time, months of notes had faces attached to them.

Expressions. Voices. Eyes.

The rain gradually softened.

Aashna looked at the sky. Then at him. A familiar mischievous smile appeared on her face.

"See?"

"What?"

"I told you."

Rishikesh already knew what was coming.

Aashna pointed toward the rain-soaked road around them.

"Destiny."

For once, he didn't argue.

Because standing beside her, with rain falling all around them, it felt very difficult not to believe in it.

CHAPTER SIX

More Than Poetry

Rishikesh spent the entire night replaying the previous afternoon in his head. The rain. The tea. The puppies. Aashna. Every time he closed his eyes, he saw her smile. By morning, he had convinced himself that he was being ridiculous.

Then, after his lecture ended, he found himself walking towards the hallway. He had barely turned the corner of the corridor when someone bumped straight into him.

"Ouch!" the girl exclaimed, clutching the books against her chest.

Rishikesh looked up and immediately smiled. "Aashna?"

She tucked a loose strand of hair behind her ear and adjusted her dupatta in haste. "Sorry, I didn't see you. I'm getting late."

Rishikesh frowned playfully. "Late? Why do you look like you're running a marathon?"

"I have a lecture in fifteen minutes."

"So?"

"So I need to reach there before the professor does."

Rishikesh folded his arms dramatically. "Relax, Miss Responsible. The classroom is literally two minutes away."

Aashna looked at him suspiciously.

"Which means," he continued proudly, "we still have thirteen whole minutes."

She laughed softly. "And what exactly are we supposed to do in thirteen minutes?"

Rishikesh pretended to think hard. "Hmm... I will try my best to make you laugh."

Aashna raised an eyebrow. "Why?"

"Because," he pointed at her face, "you always look so serious. I don't think I've ever seen you smile properly."

She shook her head. "A smile is precious. Why waste it unnecessarily?"

Rishikesh widened his eyes in fake admiration. "Wow. I have been living for years and never received such noble wisdom."

Aashna couldn't help but smile. "You are impossible."

"And you're impossible to impress."

She rolled her eyes. "Will you stop teasing me or should I just leave?"

"No, no!" Rishikesh immediately stood in front of her. "Stay."

Aashna crossed her arms.

"But tell me one thing. Why do you get angry so easily?"

"Oh, it comes naturally when I meet people like you."

Rishikesh placed a hand dramatically over his heart and blushed. "People like me? Excuse me, what does that mean?"

Aashna tilted her head, trying to suppress her laughter. "That was an insult, dumbo."

For a moment, Rishikesh simply stared at her. The smile, the teasing in her eyes, the softness in her voice.

And suddenly he realised something terrifying. He liked making her smile far more than he should.

Before he could say anything else, the college bell rang loudly.

Aashna's eyes widened. "Oh God!"

She hurried backwards, clutching her books. "Bye, Rishi!"

And before he could stop her, she was already walking away through the bustling corridor. Rishikesh stood there watching her disappear into the crowd, smiling to himself like an idiot.

"Thirteen minutes," he murmured. "Definitely not enough."

That became their first fifteen-minute conversation. Then another the next day, and another the day after that.

Soon, Rishikesh knew her schedule better than his own. Her first lecture began fifteen minutes after his last one ended.

Just fifteen minutes, but those fifteen minutes somehow became the most important part of his day. He spent hours sitting through lectures he barely remembered, checking the clock every now and then. At 8:00 a.m., he would think about the fifteen minutes. At noon, he would think about the fifteen minutes. Even during his final lecture, while professors discussed theories and formulas, part of his mind would already be beneath the old tree.

Waiting.

Sometimes they talked about books, sometimes poetry, sometimes their professors and sometimes absolutely nothing important. Yet those conversations stayed with him long after the day ended.

One afternoon, Aashna arrived carrying three books pressed against her chest. "You know," she said, "most people wait for weekends."

Rishikesh smiled. "Most people don't get fifteen minutes with their favourite person every day."

For the first time, Aashna was left speechless.

The bell rang but neither acknowledged it. A second bell followed.

Aashna shook her head. "You're going to get into trouble one day."

"Worth it."

"For fifteen minutes?"

Rishikesh looked at her. "No" his smile softened. "For you."

For a moment, the noise of the campus seemed to disappear. Then students rushed past them, breaking the silence. Aashna looked away first.

And for the rest of the day, Rishikesh couldn't stop smiling.

The next morning, he began waiting for those fifteen minutes all over again.

One day, The last bell of his lecture rang. Instinctively, Rishikesh glanced at his watch.

Eight minutes, eight more minutes before he could see Aashna. A smile found its way to his face, as always. He was halfway to the banyan tree when he spotted her. She was already there, not rushing, simply sitting beneath the tree with a book in her lap.

Rishikesh stopped "Aren't you supposed to be in class?"

Aashna closed her book, "Our professor didn't come."

For a moment, he simply stared. Then a grin spread across his face, a dangerous grin.

Aashna immediately narrowed her eyes. "Why do you look so happy?"

"Because" he said, taking the seat beside her, "For the first time in weeks, I don't have to keep checking the time every thirty seconds."

She laughed. "You make ut sound like you're serving a prison sentence, fifteen minutes is a prison sentence for you."

"It's not. It is when the person you want to talk to, who is as beautiful as gazals of Jagjit Singh to be precise.. leaves exactly when the conversation becomes interesting."

A faint blush appeared on her face. Rishikesh noticed, and silently congratulated whichever professor had decided not to show up.

For the next few minutes, neither spoke. For once there was no hurry, no bell waiting to interrupt them, no countdown running in the back of their minds.

Just time, an unfamiliar luxury.

"So," Aashna asked, "What would you do if you had an entire hour with me?"

Rishikesh pretended to think. "I'll ask you all the questions you never answer."

She groaned "Terrible start."

"What's your dream?" Rishikesh asked.

Aashna's eyes lit up instantly. That alone gave him the answer. "I want to write."

"You already do."

"No." She shook her head. "I want people across the country to read my words." Her gaze drifted somewhere beyond the road. "Maybe even beyond the country." The smile on her face softened. "I want my stories to stay with people after they finish reading them."

Rishikesh watched her speak.

The passion in her voice was impossible to miss.

"What about you?" she asked.

He thought for a moment. "I don't know."

"You don't know?"

"I've never thought that far ahead."

Aashna laughed. "That's terrifying."

"Thank you."

"No, seriously." She pointed at him. "Everyone should have a dream."

The conversation flowed naturally after that. Neither knew how much time had passed. The discussion drifted from childhood stories to favourite books and from embarrasing moments to dreams that are too big to say aloud. Now, they were not exchanging words through notes.. they were exchanging pieces of themselves.

And somewhere between laughter and stories, an hour slipped away. Neither noticed, until the bell rang.

Aashna looked at her watch and widened her eyes. "Oh no!"

"What happened?"

"I need to rush or I'll miss my next lecture."

Rishikesh burst out laughing.

For months, fifteen minutes had felt enough. Now even an hour felt too short.

At that moment, he realized something, He enjoyed listening to her. Not because she was talking about writing. Not because she was talking about dreams. Just because she was talking. He realised he could drown himself in the ocean of her words and still be alive with the bolster of her eyes.

The following days developed a rhythm of their own. A routine neither of them discussed. Yet both followed faithfully. They met after classes. Shared tea. Argued about books. Fed the puppies. Walked through crowded streets discussing everything and nothing.

One afternoon, Aashna discovered that Rishikesh could cook. The discovery happened after she complained about the hostel food for fifteen consecutive minutes. The next day he brought lunch. She stared at the container.

"You made this?"

"Unfortunately."

After tasting it, she pointed a spoon at him. "You've been hiding this talent."

"It wasn't a talent."

"It absolutely is."

The lunches became regular after that. Some days beneath trees. Some days on empty benches. Some days inside the library when the weather refused to cooperate.

Slowly, conversations became comfort. Comfort became habit. And habit became the favourite part of his day.

One evening, as the sun disappeared behind the hills, they walked through the college grounds. Students rushed around them. Someone played music from a distant hostel window. The world carried on as usual. Aashna was telling a story.

"....then the aunty in my neighbourhood started staring at me, but I stood with my ground... though later got scolded by my mother.."

Rishikesh wasn't listening. Not properly. He was watching the way her eyes brightened when she spoke. The way she laughed at her own jokes. The way she used her hands while explaining things.

Aashna suddenly stopped. "Are you even listening?"

Rishikesh blinked. "What?"

"Exactly." She folded her arms. "I knew it."

He laughed. "I was listening."

"Then what was I saying?"

Rishikesh opened his mouth. Nothing came out.

Aashna looked victorious. "I rest my case." She continued walking ahead. "Don't talk to me"

Rishikesh followed. "Achha sorry naa" A smile lingered on his face long after. At that moment, he still believed she was just a friend. He had no idea that somewhere between sticky notes, shared lunches and evening walks...

Aashna had quietly become much more than poetry.

CHAPTER SEVEN

The Void

Love did not arrive all at once, It arrived quietly. Like evening sunlight slipping through a window. Like a song playing softly in another room. Like a habit so familiar that one day you suddenly realize you cannot live without it.

For Rishikesh, it arrived somewhere between shared lunches and evening walks. Between unfinished conversations and borrowed books. Between waiting for the whole day just to see her for fifteen minutes and searching for her face in crowded hallways.

At first, he ignored it, Then denied it, Then accepted it. And once he accepted it, there was no escape.

He was in love with Aashna, hopelessly, completely, ridiculously. The realization terrified him. For weeks, he carried the confession inside him. Every day he planned to tell her. Every day he lost his courage. The words sounded perfect in his head. Yet whenever she stood in front of him, smiling as though the world had never hurt her, those words abandoned him.

That night, Rishikesh rewrote the letter three times. The first draft felt too dramatic, the second felt too cowardly but the third one felt honest.

He wrote everything he had spent months trying not to feel. About the notes, about the library cupboard, about the fifteen minutes that had somehow become the most important part of his day. He began writing.

"Dear Aashna,

I have gathered all the courage in the world to write this letter. I want to take care of you-not as a companion, not as a friend, but as someone who means something to you. I want to be the person you can trust with your happiest moments and your most vulnerable ones. I want to be the person who stays when everything else falls apart, I want to protect you, to hold your hand through every storm life sends your way. I want to be more than just friends.

- Yours Rishikesh"

When he finally folded the letter, dawn was already creeping through his window. The next morning, the envelope remained safely tucked inside his bag. His heart, however, felt anything but safe.

All through his last lecture, he rehearsed what he would say. Perhaps he would hand her the letter and leave, perhaps he would stand there and let her read it, or perhaps he would pretend it was just another poem.

The possibilities kept changing, only one thing remained certain. Today, he would finally tell her.

The bell rang.

Rishikesh hurried towards the banyan tree.

Aashna wasn't there.

He checked his watch. Five minutes passed, then ten, then fifteen. The place beneath the tree remained empty.

"Maybe she's late," he told himself. But she never came. The next day, he waited again, and even the day after that.

Nothing.

The letter remained inside his bag. Folded, unopened, unsent.

After a week, concern replaced disappointment. Rishikesh found himself wandering near the Arts Block between lectures. Searching, waiting and hoping. The class ended and the hallway was crowded with the departure of students, his eyes searched for aashna, scanning every faces but unable to find her, eventually the hallway got empty. Lastly a guy came out of the class, rishikesh immediately approached him.

"Hey, do you know where's Aashna? I am her friend Rishikesh"

"Uh, Hi! Aashna has not been attending classes past four days.. the teacher was asking about her as well, nobody knows." the guy replied. "well she has a bestfriend, she might know, but I am not aware of her name."

"Ah, thanks." rishikesh replied. he thought she might be sick, but another day passed, then another, Still no sign of her.

The bench where they usually ate lunch remained empty. The tea stall felt strangely unfamiliar. Even the puppies seemed to search for someone. Rishikesh laughed at himself for thinking that. Yet somehow the thought remained.

That evening, Rishikesh opened his bag and stared at the envelope. The edges had begun to crease from being carried everywhere. He ran his thumb across her name. Months earlier, Aashna had turned a stranger into the most familiar person in his life and now she had vanished. The letter remained where it was. Tucked safely inside his bag.

Unread by the girl who had inspired every word written on those pages

The fifteen minutes he waited for each day never arrived. For the first time in months, he found himself walking alone, The evening walks felt different now, Incomplete. Every familiar place carried traces of her. The library, The tea stall, The corner bench beneath the old tree. Everywhere he looked, there was an absence shaped exactly like Aashna.

CHAPTER EIGHT

Dance Competition

A month passed to the beginning of second year.

The excitement among the students returned when the administration announced its biggest competition of the year—an inter-college dance contest. Posters appeared across every corridor.

The winning team would receive a substantial cash prize, but that wasn't what caught everyone's attention. The highlight of the competition was a high-energy duet dance. For most students, it was exciting.

For Rishikesh, it was background noise. Ever since Aashna's disappearance, very little seemed important.

The preparation arrived with its usual chaos. Classrooms suddenly became rehearsal rooms, notice boards filled with event schedules and every corridor echoed with music from one practice session or another.

Mrunal had signed up for the duet dance competition months ago. Along with her teammates, she spent every evening practicing for the upcoming fest.

Everything was going according to plan. Until one unfortunate afternoon. During a rehearsal, her dance partner landed awkwardly after a lift. The pain was immediate. The verdict from the doctor was even more immediate.

A minor ankle fracture, no dancing for several weeks. Which meant no competition. At least for him.

For Mrunal, however, the real problem had just begun. The registration deadline had already passed and performance was barely two weeks away. Finding a replacement partner at the last moment was proving nearly impossible.

One evening, after watching her reject yet another unsuitable candidate, a senior finally laughed. "You know, there's one person who might actually save your performance."

Mrunal looked up hopefully. "Who?"

"Rishikesh."

She frowned. "The Finance Department guy?"

"The same."

"I've never even spoken to him."

"Doesn't matter. He's performed before. Picks up choreography quickly. And unlike the others, he actually shows up for practice."

Mrunal considered it. The name sounded familiar. She had seen him around campus, usually with a book in his hand, usually lost in thought. Not exactly the image of someone who enjoyed dancing which made her even more skeptical.

"Where do I find him?"

"Try the courtyard. That's usually where he disappears."

Later that evening, Mrunal spotted him. He sat alone on a bench near the library, flipping through a book. The golden evening light highlighted the sharp angles of his face.

He looked serious, Focused. The sort of person who preferred silence over unnecessary conversation.

Mrunal adjusted the strap of her bag and walked towards him.

"Rishikesh?"

He looked up. "Yes?"

"Can I talk to you for a minute?"

He nodded politely. Mrunal explained everything, the dance competition, her partner's injury, the approaching deadline. And finally, the senior who had suggested his name.

When she finished, Rishikesh remained silent for a moment.

Then he shook his head. "I‘m sorry." The answer came so quickly that she almost thought he hadn’t listened. "I can’t help you."

"Oh." Disappointment flashed across her face. "You dance, don’t you?"

"A little."

"Then why not?"

Rishikesh looked away. The truth was he wasn’t interested in dancing or he wasn’t interested in the fest, competitions, or celebrations. Lately, he wasn’t interested in much of anything.

"I’m just not the right person," he said quietly.

Mrunal tried again. The fest was important, the team had practiced for months. She was running out of options but his answer didn’t change.

"I‘m sorry."

And that was the end of the conversation.

Or so he thought.

The next day, as he stepped out of class, he nearly walked straight into her. Mrunal stood in front of him, arms crossed, determined.

Rishikesh sighed. "You again?"

"You still haven’t found me a partner."

"That sounds like your problem."

"It becomes your problem if you keep refusing."

For the first time in days, a faint smile tugged at the corner of his lips. Mrunal noticed it immediately, progress.

"Look," she continued, "I’m not asking you to win the competition."

"Then?"

"I‘m asking you to save me from public humiliation."

He laughed despite himself. Mrunal pointed at him triumphantly.

"There. You laughed. That means you’re in a better mood than yesterday."

Rishikesh shook his head. "You’ve known me for exactly two minutes."

"Three, actually."

He couldn't help smiling again. For a moment, he noticed something he hadn't yesterday. The exhaustion behind her confidence, the desperation she was trying hard to hide. She wasn't being stubborn but she was genuinely out of options.

"Please," she said softly this time.

"No dramatic speeches. No emotional blackmail."

"Good."

"Just one rehearsal."

He raised an eyebrow. "One?"

"One."

"You promise?"

"I promise."

Rishikesh knew she was lying. They both knew she was lying. A long silence followed.

Finally, he exhaled. "Fine."

Mrunal blinked. "Fine?"

"One rehearsal."

The grin that appeared on her face could probably be seen from the other end of the campus. Before he could change his mind, she extended her hand. "Thank you."

Rishikesh shook it reluctantly.

He had agreed only because she looked completely defeated. At least that's what he told himself.

As she walked away, victorious, her gaze lingered on him for a moment longer than necessary. There was something about him, calm, composed and despite his constant attempts to avoid attention, undeniably handsome.

A strange flutter stirred inside her stomach, she ignored it.

Their first rehearsal began the next day.

The dance studio was nearly empty except for the low hum of the speakers. Mrunal connected her phone to the sound system and turned around with excitement sparkling in her eyes.

"Ready?"

"Not even remotely."

"Good enough."

The music started.

Mrunal stepped closer and guided his hand towards her waist.

Rishikesh visibly stiffened.

She couldn't help laughing.

"You know, I don't bite."

"I'm trying not to mess up the hold, nothing personal."

But somehow it felt perssonal, the careful distance he maintained, the way he avoided lingering eye contact, the way he seemed present physically while his thoughts were somewhere else entirely.

Mrunal noticed it.

CHAPTER NINE

The Growing Feelings

The following rehearsal on the next day,

During practice, she lost her footing during a spin, before she could fall, a strong arm wrapped around her waist and the other steadied her wrist. For a span of second everything seemed to stop, the music faded, the conversation hung in the air and the room exceptionally silent. Their eyes met.

Mrunal's breath caught, Rishikesh looked equally surprised by their closeness.

"You alright?" he asked softly, helping her with the foot movements

"Yeah."

Her voice came out quieter than intended.

He immediately helped her regain balance and stepped back, The distance returned. As if the moment had never happened. But for some reason, Mrunal found herself thinking about it long after rehearsal ended.

And Rishikesh? his thoughts remained somewhere else, lost in a girl who had vanished without a trace.

Unaware that while he was waiting for someone from his past to return... Someone else had quietly begun walking into his future.

With weeks of practices, countless arguments and hours spent together, the day of final rehearsal had come.

It was past 9 PM, the campus nearly empty, but the auditorium lights were still on. They moved in sync now, their steps smooth and their rythm sharp. Rishikesh was more relaxed this days - still quiet, still careful, but his smile came easier around her

They've been practising since the morning, drastically tired. After the final take, Mrunal collapsed on the floor dramatically. "If we don't win, I am suing the judges"

Rishikesh sat beside her, offering his water bottle "You're too competitive"

"You're too unbothered" she countered sipping "Balance"

He nodded thoughtfully "We make a good team"

The words sat warm in her chest. She glanced sideways at him, the peace in his eyes, the way his hairs curled slightly at the edges when he sweat, memorised in her head like a scenery she never wanted to forget.

She liked him, She didn't planned to- but she did.

He looked back at her and smiled, she smiled too because even if he didn't see her the way she saw him, she still wanted to stay close.

"See you at 10 a.m. tomorrow" she said "Don't be late"

He nodded as he picked up his backpack to go.

While heading back to the hostel he saw varun running towards him. "Bro there's a letter for you" he took a breath. "Someone was waiting for you but you didn't come so they dropped a letter our hostel's gatekeeper"

He immediately took the letter from Varun's hand and tore it open carefully. the paper inside was soft and the handwriting, unmistakeable.

"Hey Rishikesh!

I know I've disappeared without a word, I had my reasons. Can you meet me at Triveni Ghat tomorrow morning? I'll be there by 5:45 a.m. There's a sunrise waiting and I think we should watch it together.

- Aashna"

For a moment, the words blurred, his eyes stayed fixed on the letter, reading it again and again, as if afraid it might vanish if he blinked.

Aashna. After nearly a month of silence

He leaned back against the window, his lips pulling into az rare, genuine smile. Not the one he gave at dance rehearsal, not the forced one at club meetings, this one was different- unfiltered, hopeful.

"Who is it?" Varun asked.

"Aashna, she wants to meet tomorrow"

"But tomorrow is your performance" Varun sighed

"I'll be back by then, Can't miss this chance to meet her" Rishikesh replied

The world felt lighter, his steps back to the room had a bounce he hadn't felt in weeks. And that night as he lay on his bed staring at the ceiling sleep came slow, wrapped in anticipation. Tomorrow he would see her again and maybe, just maybe, everything would make sense.

CHAPTER TEN

The Confession

Sleep became impossible that night, After weeks of searching for traces of her in empty classrooms and forgotten corners of the campus, after weeks of silence, Aashna had finally written back.

Every time he closed his eyes, he imagined the meeting. What would he say? Would she explain where she had been? Had she read his letter? Was she angry? Would things go back to how they were? Or had everything changed?

By the time dawn arrived, he had already been awake for hours.

At 5:35 a.m., Rishikesh stood at Triveni Ghat. Ten minutes early.

The river flowed quietly beside him, The sky still carried traces of darkness. A cool breeze drifted across the water. Around him, devotees prepared for the morning prayers while the city slowly awakened.

Normally, Rishikesh hated waiting. Today, every second felt longer than the last. His fingers repeatedly checked his watch.

5:38, 5:40, 5:42.

His heart seemed determined to beat faster with every passing minute.

Then he saw her.

Walking towards him through the soft morning mist. For a moment, the entire world fell silent.

Aashna.

She wore a light shawl draped over her shoulders, The early morning breeze played with her hair, leaving a few strands dancing across her face. The rising sun painted the horizon gold behind her. And somehow, standing there between the river and the morning light, she looked almost unreal, Almost ethereal.

Rishikesh forgot every sentence he had rehearsed. Forgot every question he had prepared. Forgot how to speak. He simply stared, As if afraid she might disappear again.

Aashna stopped a few feet away, A faint smile touched her lips.

"Hi."

The word finally broke the spell.

Rishikesh exhaled. "Where have you been?"

The question escaped immediately. Without any greeting or small talk, just a question that had haunted him for weeks.

Aashna looked down for a moment, Then smiled sadly. "Long story."

"Do you know how afraid I was overthinking every single day if you're alright or not?"

Silence settled between them. Not uncomfortable, Just heavy.

"I heard you're performing today," she said. "I wasn't sure you'd come."

Rishikesh shook his head. A small smile appeared on his face. "Nothing makes more sense than watching a sunrise with you."

For the first time that morning, Aashna laughed softly. The sound felt familiar, Like coming home after being lost.

They stood beside the river as the first rays of sunlight spread across the water. For a few moments, neither spoke.

Then Rishikesh realized something. He had spent weeks waiting for this moment. If he left now without saying what he came to say, he would regret it forever. Blood started rushing to his cheeks, his palm suddenly felt warm. But he forced himself to continue.

"Aashna..."

She turned towards him.

Rishikesh took a deep breath. Then another. And finally said the words he had carried for months.

"Aashna, I'm in love with you."

The river continued flowing, birds flew across the sky, the world remained unchanged. Yet for him, everything had changed.

"Every inch of my heart belongs to you." His voice trembled slightly "I've tried to tell myself it's just friendship."A small laugh escaped him "It isn't." he looked directly into her eyes "Your absence made me realize how deeply I crave your presence."

Aashna remained silent, not because she wanted him to stop, but because she couldn't look away.

Rishikesh continued "I want to be beside you, for now and for the rest of my life."

The words hung between them, fragile but honest.

Aashna's eyes glistened slightly in the morning light, still, she said nothing.

Rishikesh smiled, A nervous smile. The kind that appears when someone has finally placed their heart in another person's hands.

"If your answer is no, I'll respect it." He took a step back

"But if it's yes..." Aashna looked up "...show up to my performance today."

A faint breeze swept across the ghat. Rishikesh smiled again.

"If that happens, If you said yes, I'll probably spend the rest of my life thanking the gods of every religion, Which is saying a lot, considering I'm an atheist."

That finally earned a laugh from her, a real one. The kind he had missed.

Rishikesh glanced at his watch, his performance was approaching. Reluctantly, he began stepping away saying "I'll wait for you, Aashna"

Aashna watched him go.

He stopped once, turned back as though wanting to memorize the sight of her standing there. Then he smiled and walked away.

Leaving behind his confession.

CHAPTER ELEVEN

PERFORMANCE DAY

Backstage was chaos.

Students rushed from one corner to another carrying props, costumes and last-minute instructions. Music from different performances echoed through the auditorium walls.

Mrunal stood near the curtain, checking the entrance gate almost hundred times. Her irritation was quickly turning into panic. Their performance was less than twenty minutes away.

"Where is he?" she muttered.

She checked the entrance again, still no sign of Rishikesh. For the first time since joining the competition, she felt genuinely nervous, not because of the dance, not because of the audience, because of what she planned to do afterward. She had rehearsed the words countless times in her head. If they won, she would tell him. Even If they lost, she would still tell him. Either way, she was done hiding her feelings. The only problem was that the idiot hasn't arrived yet.

"Unbelievable," she groaned "I'm going to kill him."

Almost on cue, Rishikesh appeared backstage, breathing slightly heavily. As though he had run half the city to get there.

Mrunal marched straight toward him. "Are you out of your mind?"

Rishikesh blinked "What?"

"What do you mean what? We perform in twenty minutes!"

"I know."

She looked ready to throw her water bottle at him.

"Get ready. Right now."

Rishikesh apologized, though his smile refused to disappear.

Mrunal narrowed her eyes "You look suspiciously happy."

"Do I?"

"Yes."

His smile widened.

Mrunal sighed dramatically.

"Whatever happened, save it for later. Right now, we dance."

The auditorium lights dimmed and the announcer called their names, a roar of applause filled the hall. The music began, smooth, sensual, pulsing with rythm. for the next few minutes, everything disappeared.

Mrunal and Rishikesh stepped onto the stage with other teammates, the first beat hit, and they moved- synchronised, fluid, every step an echo of the hours they'd poured into rehearsals, every spin landed perfectly. every lift flowed smoothly. The crowd cheered louder with each passing second.

As the final note echoed through the auditorium, thunderous applause erupted. Breathing heavily, they exchanged a glance, mrunal smiled, her heart racing- not just from the dance but from being in this moment with him.

The final hit- her arms extended, his hold firm drew grasps from the audience with the erruption of appaluse.

An hour later, all the participating teams stood on stage waiting for the results. The tension was unbearable, Mrunal squeezed her hands together nervously. Rishikesh, meanwhile, kept scanning the audience, Row after row, Face after face, searching and waiting.

The announcer finally approached the microphone "The winners of this year's Inter-College Dance Fest are..."

A pause.

"Team Roar led by Mrunal and Rishikesh!"

The auditorium exploded. Mrunal let out a scream of excitement "We won!" Before Rishikesh could react, she had already pulled him into a celebratory hug.

A large trophy was placed in their hands, Cameras flashed, number of students surrounded them. Everyone was celebrating except Rishikesh.

Not because he wasn't happy, but because his eyes continued searching every row and every corner that existed looking for one person, Aashna, but she wasn't there and his mind overanalysing everything he said in the morning.

As the celebrations continued around him, disappointment slowly settled inside his chest, Maybe she hadn't come, maybe her answer was no, maybe the sunrise confession had meant nothing.

The trophy suddenly felt much lighter than it should have.

The crowd began dispersing, students left their seats, parents gathered near the exits, performers posed for photographs, rishikesh stood quietly near the edge of the stage.

Then he saw her, near the auditorium's exit standing beside the door, watching him.

Aashna.

For a second, he thought he was imagining things, then she smiled and the entire world came rushing back. Without thinking, he handed the trophy to someone nearby and sprinted. Ignoring the stairs would have been dangerous. Taking them normally would have been impossible. He rushed down them as fast as he could and crossed the distance between them.

"Aashna..."

Before she could say anything, he pulled her into a hug, a tight one, the kind that carries months of waiting, months of fear, months of unanswered questions.

For a moment, neither moved, neither wanted to.

Then Aashna laughed softly "So..."

Rishikesh looked at her.

She tilted her head. "Which god are you thanking first?"

He froze. Then burst into laughter.

The same laugh she had missed hearing.

"You have no idea how happy I am today."

"The trophy?"

Rishikesh shook his head. "No."

His eyes never left hers.

"Not because I won the trophy." A pause "Because I won you."

Aashna looked away shyly, A faint blush appeared on her face. Then she suddenly narrowed her eyes.

"Wait."

"What?"

"You never told me you were performing with Mrunal."

Rishikesh frowned "Hold on." His confusion deepened "You know Mrunal?"

Aashna looked equally surprised "Of course I do."

"How?"

"She's my best friend, idiot."

Rishikesh stared, Then laughed.

"You're kidding."

"I'm not."

Both laughed at the absurdity of it. The world suddenly seemed much smaller and much kinder.

From the balcony above, Mrunal watched everything. The celebration, the hug, the smile on Rishikesh's face she had never seen before, the way he looked at Aashna.

As though nothing else existed, and suddenly, everything made sense. The distance he always maintained, the absent-mindedness, the sadness she sometimes caught in his eyes.

It had never been about dance or rehearsals. His heart had belonged to someone else all along.

A single tear escaped before she could stop it, she quickly wiped it away. No one noticed. Neither of them noticed. Perhaps that was for the best.

Down below, Rishikesh and Aashna were smiling at each other as though the rest of the world had disappeared.

Mrunal looked away, then quietly turned toward the exit, Leaving the auditorium before either of them could see her.

And for the first time that evening, the trophy no longer felt like the biggest thing that had been won—or lost.

CHAPTER TWELVE

Silent Battles

The celebration continued long after the auditorium had emptied, students clicked photographs, friends exchanged congratulations. The winning trophy passed from one hand to another.

Yet none of it mattered much to Rishikesh, because for the first time in weeks, Aashna was beside him, and she wasn't leaving. As the evening faded into night, the two walked together towards the girls' hostel. The campus looked different after dark, the pathways were quieter, the crowds had disappeared, only the occasional streetlamp illuminated their way.

For a while, neither spoke, they simply enjoyed the comfort of each other's company, The comfort they had missed for far too long.

Finally, Rishikesh broke the silence "Can I ask you something?"

Aashna smiled "You always do."

"Why did you disappear?"

The smile faded, Rishikesh immediately regretted asking.

But Aashna shook her head "No. You deserve to know."

For a few moments, she remained quiet, as if arranging painful memories into words. Then she began "I come from a small village called Aragam in Kashmir." Rishikesh listened carefully "My family is... traditional." She laughed softly, a bitter laugh "Actually, traditional is probably a very polite word." The humor disappeared from her voice "Most girls there are married by my age."

Rishikesh frowned.

"And college?"

"Difficult."

"And writing?"

Aashna looked at him and smiled sadly "Impossible."

They continued walking.

"The only reason I came here was because of my grandfather." her eyes softened immediately "Dadujaan." The word itself carried affection.

"He always believed in me."

"He supported your studies?"

"More than that." A faint smile appeared.

"He was the first person who ever read my poems."

Rishikesh couldn't help smiling "He sounds wonderful."

"He is."

Aashna looked ahead "If it wasn't for him, I would've never left Kashmir."

The silence returned, this time heavier.

"My father never wanted me to study literature."

Rishikesh noticed she deliberately said father instead of dad, as though there was distance hidden inside the word.

"He wanted me to finish my degree and get married."

"And when he found out about writing?"

Aashna laughed again, the sound carried no happiness.

"He hated it."

"What?"

"He believes women who write become too bold."

Rishikesh stopped walking "That's ridiculous."

"I know." She continued walking.

"He took away whatever savings I had."

The anger rose instantly inside him "Why?"

"Because I was trying to publish my work."

Rishikesh looked at her in disbelief "You were actually trying to publish a book?"

A shy smile appeared "Just a small collection of poems."

"That's incredible."

"Apparently not according to him."

The smile disappeared again.

"When he found out, he came to campus himself." The memory clearly hurt "He packed my things and took me back home."

The night air felt colder.

"And you couldn't contact anyone?"

Aashna shook her head

The realization hit Rishikesh all at once. The unanswered letters, the silence, the disappearance. None of it had been her choice.

"Aashna..." his voice softened.

She looked away "He isn't my real father." the words came out quietly, barely above a whisper.

Rishikesh froze. "What?"

"My stepfather." A tear escaped before she could stop it, she quickly wiped it away. but another followed, then another. "I've spent most of my life trying not to disappoint him." Her voice trembled "And no matter what I do, it's never enough."

Rishikesh felt his chest tighten.

"There were days when writing was the only thing that made me feel like myself." she laughed weakly.

"Sounds dramatic, doesn't it?"

"No." he answered immediately "It doesn't."

For the first time that evening, she looked directly into his eyes, and saw no judgment. Only understanding.

"My house was never really a home."

The confession hung between them, raw, honest and painful.

"My mother tried her best." Aashna whispered "But Dadujaan..." she paused "He is the only person who ever made me feel safe."

Another tear rolled down her cheek. Before she could wipe it away, Rishikesh gently wiped her tears and held her hands, like he was holding something very precious, something very fragile. The gesture carried more comfort than any speech could.

"You still have him." She nodded "Yes."

"And now?" Aashna looked at their joined hands.

Rishikesh squeezed them gently giving her a silent reassurance, a promise that now no matter what hardships life sends to her he will never leave her side, not in this lifetime.

Aashna smiled through her tears "And now..." she whispered "I have you too."

For a moment, neither spoke. the lights glowed softly around them, the night breeze rustled through the trees. And for the first time in a very long time, Aashna felt something she rarely allowed herself to feel, to hope. Not because her struggles were over or life had suddenly become easy, But because she no longer had to carry them alone.

As they reached the hostel gate, Rishikesh looked at her and smiled "You know, one day your book will be published."

Aashna laughed "You sound very confident."

"I am."

"What if it doesn't happen?"

Rishikesh shook his head "It will."

"How do you know?"

He smiled "Because if destiny was stubborn enough to make us meet through sticky notes, rainstorms, disappearances..."

Aashna laughed "...then?"

"...then it would be foolish enough to make your dream come true too."

For the first time in months, Aashna laughed without sadness hiding behind it, and that sound stayed with Rishikesh long after she disappeared behind the hostel gates.

On the other side,

The curtains hadn't been drawn in days. Mrunal lay curled up beneath a blanket. She had not gone to class, She barely spoke to anyone. When her mother knocked in the door she claimed she had a headache. The trophy sat on her desk across the room, untouched, collecting dust. She laid in silence. But inside? It was loud.

She remembered how quickly Rishikesh walked past her, "He didn't even look back"

That hurt more than she would ever admit. And right now, all she wanted was to be unseen.

It was late afernoon, Mrunal's mother barged into her room, gently patting on her head she asked "Are you alright Mrunu?" her voice full of concern.

Mrunal whispered "Just tired Maa"

Her mother didn't question the lie. Instead, she said "I don't know what's suffering you right now, beta. But life doesn't stop for one person or one moment. You were never meant to hide from the world- you were meant to light it up"

Mrunal blinked away tears.

She returned to class the next week. And slowly, the noise of college life began to pull her back.

CHAPTER THIRTEEN

DAYS OF HAPPINESS

The next morning, Rishikesh was waiting outside the hostel gate before Aashna arrived. She smiled the moment she saw him, his eyes lit up in a way a parched persons's eyes does with the sight of water

"You came early."

"You said bookstore."

"As if that explains anything."

"It explains everything."

Aashna laughed and shook her head. Together, they walked through the busy streets until they reached the old bookstore tucked between two crowded shops. The moment they stepped inside, Aashna transformed. She moved from shelf to shelf, picking up books with the excitement of a child entering a toy store, sometimes she read the blurbs carefully, sometimes she flipped through random pages, sometimes she smiled, sometimes she frowned, sometimes her eyes widened with excitement.

Rishikesh wasn't paying attention to the books anymore, he was watching her.

One could tell entire stories just by looking at her expressions.

A strand of hair slipped across her face as she reached for a novel, without thinking, Rishikesh stepped closer and gently he tucked the strand behind her ear.

Aashna froze.

Their eyes met.

For a moment, neither moved, neither spoke.

The noise of the bookstore seemed to disappear. The world shrank to a few inches between them. Aashna's fingers lightly grasped the collar of his shirt, Rishikesh felt his heartbeat stumble. She was close enough for him to hear her breathing. Close enough to forget every coherent thought.

Their meetings slowly became a ritual, a part of everyday life, a habit neither questioned. Lunches turned into hours of conversation, walks became effortless, goodbyes became harder and hugs became longer. Sometimes they shared a single cup of tea, sometimes they argued about books, sometimes they sat together doing absolutely nothing. And somehow, those moments became their favorites. Life felt lighter, happier.

As if the world had finally decided to be kind.

One evening, they sat together in a quiet park overlooking the setting sun. The sun spilled its golden light across the grass and to Rishikesh's brown eyes which somehow looked golden, deep and breathtaking. The sky glowed with shades of orange and pink, neither felt the need to speak much

The children played in the distance, annoying as usual, "who even likes children" Rishikesh murmured

Aashna laughed him off and suddenly patted her lap.

Rishikesh blinked "What?"

"Come here."

His ears immediately turned red "Aashna..."

She raised an eyebrow "Are you scared?"

"No."

"Then come here."

Muttering something about emotional blackmail, Rishikesh finally rested his head in her lap.

Aashna smiled triumphantly "There."

The breeze moved softly through the trees. For a while, she slowly ran her fingers through his hair. Her touch was gentle, the way one comforts someone they care deeply about. Rishikesh closed his eyes, a strange sense of peace settled over him.

"I never thought I'd be this happy, Rishi." Her voice was almost a whisper.

He opened his eyes and looked up at her, the fading sunlight framed her face. For a second, she looked exactly like the dream he feared waking from.

"Me too, Aashna." his voice softened "This feels unreal."

Aashna smiled "It does."

"A dream I don't want to wake up from."

A silence followed, not the uncomfortable one, but the warm silence

"A dream I want to last forever."

For a moment, neither looked away. Then Aashna leaned down and gently kissed his forehead. It might be a simple gesture, yet it carried more affection than a thousand words.

Rishikesh smiled, for the first time in his life, he felt completely safe, understood and loved. Yes, it is a very underrated feeling to have as a guy but, with the right girl it comes inevitably.

The next afternoon, they decided to visit the place where everything had begun; the library. The building stood almost empty, only a handful of students occupied the reading tables. The familiar silence welcomed them. Together, they walked towards the old cupboard hidden in the corner, the very same cupboard that had started everything, the same cupboard that had carried poems, jokes, confessions and hope.

Aashna opened it curiously, then froze. Inside lay a fresh sunflower, bright yellow against the wooden shelf. She picked it up carefully, followed by an immediate smile.

"How?" She turned towards him "Who put this here?" Her eyes narrowed playfully "Was it you?"

Rishikesh smiled, before she could step away, he gently reached for her hand. Pulling her closer, just enough to make her heart race. Aashna laughed nervously "Rishi..."

"Yes."

"People are going to see."

"Let them."

She lightly pushed his shoulder, he refused to move. His smile only widened.

"You're impossible."

"And yet, here you are."

Aashna rolled her eyes, though her blush betrayed her. Rishikesh leaned slightly closer.

"Yes."

She looked at him.

"It was me."

"The sunflower?"

"The sunflower."

A pause.

"Your mad lover."

Aashna laughed, the sound echoed softly through the empty aisle. Then she looked down at the flower, the same flower he had once left beside a sticky note, the same flower that had quietly become theirs. For a few moments, neither spoke because words suddenly felt unnecessary.

Their hands found each other naturally, As though they belonged there, together, they walked out of the library. Their fingers remained intertwined. And for that brief chapter of life, the future seemed impossibly bright.

As though happiness would last forever.

CHAPTER FOURTEEN

ANOTHER SIDE

The afternoon had begun like any other but It ended with blood on the ground. The college football field buzzed with students enjoying the pleasant weather. Laughter echoed across the grounds. Rishikesh stood near the boundary wall talking with a few classmates when Arjun approached, A senior, more of a troublemaker, and someone Rishikesh had never particularly liked.

The exchange began with harmless remarks, then came the taunts, then came Aashna.

Arjun smirked "So where's your shadow today?"

Rishikesh frowned "What?"

"You know exactly what I mean." The senior laughed.

"That girl."

Rishikesh's expression hardened.

Arjun continued.

"The one you follow around like a lost puppy."

A few students exchanged uncomfortable glances, the smile on Arjun's face widened.

"Honestly, man." He shook his head dramatically "You run behind that third-class girl all day."

The crowd went silent. Something snapped, The next moment, Rishikesh's fist collided with Arjun's jaw. Gasps erupted around the ground. Arjun stumbled backwards before charging at him. The fight exploded, one punch after another, intense shouting, dust rising from the ground and students gathering from every direction.

Neither seemed willing to stop. Years of anger and pride collided in a matter of minutes.

Then a voice cut through the chaos.

"RISHI!"

Everything froze.

Aashna.

She pushed through the crowd. Breathless and terrified, her eyes immediately found him

The cut near his eyebrow, blood on his lip, bruised knuckles. For a moment, she couldn't speak.

This wasn't the Rishikesh she knew, this wasn't the boy who left sunflowers in library cupboards, the boy who packed lunch for her. the boy who listened to her dreams for hours, this was someone else, someone frightening.

She grabbed his arm.

"Stop."

Rishikesh looked at her, the anger disappeared almost instantly.

"Aashna—"

"No."

Her voice trembled.

"No."

She pulled him away from the crowd, away from Arjun, away from the shouting, Only when they reached a quieter corner did she finally let go.

For a few moments, neither spoke, the silence felt unbearable.

Then Aashna looked at his injuries and her eyes filled with tears.

"What were you thinking?"

Rishikesh opened his mouth but nothing came out.

"I never knew this side of you existed."

The words hurt more than any punch.

"What if something had happened to you?"

Her voice cracked.

"What if..."

She couldn't finish.

Rishikesh reached up instinctively, wanting to comfort her, wanting to wipe away her tears, wanting to hold her. But the moment his hand moved, Aashna flinched, just slightly, just for a second. Yet it felt like a knife, As though she expected him to hurt her. The realization shattered him, his hand froze midway, guilt flooded his chest.

Aashna noticed it too.. and somehow that made the tears fall harder.

"For the first time..." her voice barely rose above a whisper "I'm afraid of you, Rishi."

The words lingered between them, heavy, painful but honest.

Rishikesh looked down, unable to meet her eyes. The shame was unbearable, because she wasn't wrong. This wasn't the first fight, this wasn't even close. People knew him for this, but he never wanted her to know him for this. Never her.

"Aashna..."

His voice broke.

"I'm sorry."

She wiped her eyes.

"If you ever do this again..." A long pause "Forget me."

Rishikesh's head immediately shot up "No."

"If you ever choose violence over yourself..." Another tear escaped "I can't be part of that."

He took a step closer, carefully, slowly, making sure she knew she was safe.

"My baby." his voice was soft, almost pleading "I won't."

Aashna looked at him. searching for the traces of certainity and truth in his eyes

"Promise?"

Without hesitation, he nodded "Promise."

For a moment, neither moved.

Then Aashna finally stepped forward.

Resting her forehead lightly against his shoulder. Rishikesh closed his eyes, holding her gently. As though she were the most precious thing in the world. Because to him, she was.

Aashna then pulls out of the hug and asks "Why did you never tell me about this side of yours"

"Because it never existed when you are around" he replied without a second thought

"Are you still angry?" he looked into her eyes

"Yes I am because I love you, as fiercely as a human heart is capable of loving, seeing you like this.. all hurt and injured wrenches my heart to the core" she confessed angrily

Rishikesh shook his head, trying not to blush but failed.

"Why are you laughing, does it seems like a joke to you?" she said slightly hitting his arm

"Ouch!" he grasped after getting hit on a fresh wound

"Achha listen" he said pulling her closer "I'm really really sorry"

Anger finally made a way out of her eyes. Their foreheads rested together.

Like they depend on each other for survival.

CHAPTER FIFTEEN

A Call from Home

The afternoon had been ordinary, Until Aashna came running into Rishikesh's hostel. Rishikesh had just returned from class when he heard hurried footsteps in the corridor. Before he could react, the door burst open.

Aashna stood there, breathless and shaking. Tears were streaming down her face.

For a second, his heart stopped.

"Aashna?"

She tried to speak, but nothing came out. The moment she looked at him, she broke down completely.

Without thinking, Rishikesh crossed the room and pulled her into his arms.

"It's okay." His hand gently moved through her hair. "It's okay, Aashi."

She clutched his shirt tightly. As though she would collapse if she let go.

Rishikesh guided her to sit on the edge of the bed and sat beside her

"What happened?"

Aashna wiped her eyes, only for fresh tears to replace them.

"My hostel warden got a call." her voice trembled "A call from my father." The word father carried its usual discomfort. Rishikesh immediately felt uneasy.

"What did he say?"

Aashna's lips quivered "Dadujaan is in the hospital." The room suddenly felt quieter. "My father said his condition is critical." A tear rolled down her cheek, "They don't know if he'll recover." The words shattered her. She buried her face in her hands.

"I'm scared, Rishi." Her voice broke completely "So scared."

Rishikesh moved closer, taking her trembling hands into his own.

"He'll be alright."

"What if he isn't?"

The question came immediately, clearly raw and terrified.

"What if something happens to him?" her breathing became uneven "You don't understand." Tears continued falling "He's the only person who believed in me, the only person who never made me feel like a burden."

Rishikesh listened quietly, every word hurt like a stab in the chest. Because he knew for her dadujaan wasn't just family, he was her safe place, and safe places were rare in Aashna's life.

Aashna continued "I need to go back home, now."

Rishikesh squeezed her hands gently, "Okay, Listen to me."

Aashna looked up.

"Pack your things." he smiled softly, "And go be with him, he needs you right now"

"What if—"

"No." He shook his head "No what ifs."forcing confidence into his voice, he continued, "Your Dadujaan is going to be fine."

Aashna gave him a doubtful look "You don't know that."

"No." He admitted "But worrying yourself sick won't help him either."

For the first time since arriving, a faint smile appeared on her face. tiny, fragile. But there.

"Come on." Rishikesh stood. "Pack your things, I'll drop you to the bus stand."

"I need to meet Mrunal as well. Don't know why she has been distant since I came back.."

"She might be going through things.. Meet her if you feel like, then I'll pick you up"

Rishikesh picked her from Mrunal's house an hour later, they stood together beneath the fading evening sky. The bus stand buzzed with movement. The Vendors shouted tremendously, Passengers hurried between platforms. Buses arrived and departed in clouds of dust. Yet somehow, everything felt distant, muted. Because all Rishikesh could think about was the fact that she was leaving, again.

Aashna adjusted the strap of her bag. Neither of them knew what to say. The departure felt too sudden, too unfair. Finally, the conductor called for boarding.

Aashna looked towards the bus, then back at him.

Rishikesh's chest tightened, he hated this feeling. The helplessness, the waiting, the uncertainty. This time, however, he wasn't going to let her disappear completely.

"Aashi." She looked up "Find a way to contact me." His voice was quiet, but serious.

"Anything, A call, I have bought a Nokia, I have annoted the number at the last page of your diary."

"A letter or a message through someone."

"I don't care."

Aashna's eyes softened "Rishi..."

"I mean it." He took a step closer "Just let me know you're okay." His smile wavered "I don't think I can survive another disappearance."

Aashna laughed through her tears, the sound was bittersweet. Then she nodded "I'll try."

"No." he corrected "You'll succeed."

That earned a genuine smile. For a moment, neither moved, neither wanted to.

Then Rishikesh opened his arms, Aashna immediately stepped into them. Holding him tightly, as though memorizing the feeling, as though storing it away for difficult days ahead.

Rishikesh closed his eyes, breathing in the familiar scent of her hair. Trying to convince himself this was temporary. Just a few days or maybe a week. Nothing more.

Yet his heart felt strangely heavy.

The conductor called again, this time more impatiently. Aashna reluctantly stepped back.

Rishikesh smiled, a sad smile. "I'll miss you, Aashi." The words came out softer than intended.

Aashna's eyes immediately filled again "I'll miss you too."

One last smile, one last look. Then she boarded the bus. Rishikesh remained standing there long after it disappeared from sight, watching the empty road. Unaware that this goodbye would become far more significant than either of them imagined. Because sometimes the hardest part of a tragedy is not the ending, It's the moment when everything still feels temporary.

CHAPTER SIXTEEN

ECHOES OF SILENCE

The first day without Aashna felt manageable.

The second felt longer.

By the fourth day, Rishikesh had begun checking his phone every few minutes. Even the snake game did not feel as interesting.

He never realized how much space Aashna occupied in his life until she wasn't there. The tea stall near the college suddenly felt quieter. The library seemed unusually empty. Even the evening walks he once enjoyed now felt incomplete. Every place carried a memory of her, and every memory somehow made her absence feel heavier.

He knew why she had left. He knew she was with her family. He knew her grandfather was critically ill.

Yet knowing those things did little to comfort him.

That afternoon he sat outside the hostel with Varun, pretending to listen to whatever story his friend was telling. In reality, his eyes kept drifting towards his phone lying on the table.

Varun noticed immediately. "You've checked that thing at least twenty times in ten minutes."

Rishikesh picked it up again. "Twenty-one."

"She's been gone four days, not four years."

Rishikesh leaned back in his chair. "It feels like four years."

"You're impossible."

"That's what she says too."

The faint smile on his face disappeared almost immediately. Varun noticed but chose not to comment, The conversation died there.

A few minutes later, Rishikesh's phone suddenly vibrated. An landline number flashed across the screen of the keypad mobile. For a moment, his heart stopped, then he answered before the second ring.

"Hello?"

There was silence. Not the comfortable kind, bhe painful kind. Then came a familiar voice.

"Rishi..."

Relief washed over him instantly.

"Aashna."

But the relief lasted only a second. Something was wrong, her voice sounded broken, fragile, like someone barely holding themselves together.

"Aashi, what happened?"

On the other side of the call, he heard her breathing unevenly. Then a sob escaped her lips. The sound made his stomach drop.

"Dadujaan is no more, Rishi."

For a moment, the world around him disappeared. The chatter of students, the sound of traffic, even Varun sitting beside him. Everything faded into the background. All he could hear was Aashna crying.

The man she spoke about with so much love. The man who had encouraged her dreams when nobody else did. The man who had sent her to college despite opposition from her family.

Gone.

Rishikesh closed his eyes. He wanted to hold her, wanted to sit beside her, wanted to wipe away her tears. Instead, hundreds of kilometers separated them.

All he had was a phone call.

"I'm sorry, Aashi."

The words felt painfully small. Aashna cried harder.

"He was the only person who believed in me." Her voice trembled. "The only person who made me feel like I mattered."

Rishikesh remained silent for a moment. Sometimes grief didn't need solutions, It only needed someone willing to stay. So he listened.

For nearly half an hour he sat there while Aashna cried, spoke, remembered, and cried again. Whenever her voice broke completely, he gently encouraged her to breathe. Whenever she blamed herself for not being there sooner, he reminded her that she had done everything she could.

Slowly, the sobs became quieter. Not gone, just quieter.

When she finally calmed down, Rishikesh hesitated before asking the question that had been lingering in his mind.

"How are things at home?"

The silence that followed gave him his answer before she spoke.

"Complicated."

He understood immediately. Her father, the same man who hated her writing, the same man who had taken away her phone, the same man who wanted to control every aspect of her future.

Rishikesh looked down. "When are you coming back?"

This time the pause lasted longer.

"Two or three days."

His chest instantly felt lighter "Really?"

"Yeah." She sniffled.

"Dadujaan's final rituals are going on. Once everything is over, I'll come back."

A smile appeared on Rishikesh's face, he hadn't realized how desperately he needed to hear that.

Then Aashna added, "This is my house's landline telephone."

"What?"

"Yes I said I need to make a call for an academic emergency." despite everything, a small laugh escaped her "So don't call back."

Rishikesh smiled "Fine."

"If I can, I'll contact you again."

"I'll wait." The words slipped out naturally

Aashna fell silent, then softly whispered, "I miss you."

Rishikesh looked towards the evening sky. The words warmed his heart despite the sadness surrounding them.

"I miss you too."

Another pause, then came the words he never grew tired of hearing.

"Love you, Rishi." He smiled.

"Love you too, Aashna."

Neither disconnected immediately, neither wanted to. Eventually the call ended. For the first time in days, Rishikesh felt at peace. She was coming back, In two or three days. He could wait that long. Or so he thought.

Two days passed.

Then three.

Every morning he found himself glancing towards the college gate, expecting her familiar figure to appear at any moment.

She didn't.

He wasn't worried yet. Travel delays happened, family responsibilities happened, perhaps she needed a little more time.

Five days passed, then a week. Still nothing, no call, no message, no letter.Rishikesh began spending longer hours near the library, almost as if he expected her to appear beside him out of nowhere and laugh at how worried he had become.

One evening, he returned to his hostel room after playing volleyball. The corridor was unusually crowded. A group of students stood near the common area at the center of them stood Arjun. Rishikesh immediately recognized him, their previous altercation had become hostel gossip months ago. Neither had liked the other since.

The moment Arjun spotted him, a smirk appeared on his face. "Well, look who's here."

Rishikesh ignored him and continued walking. Unfortunately, Arjun wasn't finished.

"What's the matter these days?" No response. "You used to have a lot more attitude."

Still nothing. His friends exchanged amused glances.

Arjun stepped forward. "Or did that girl take it away with her?"

Rishikesh stopped. For the first time, the corridor grew quiet. Arjun noticed and smiled. He had found the wound.

"So it is true."

Rishikesh slowly turned around. "What did you say?"

"I said your girlfriend disappeared and suddenly you've forgotten how to talk."

The boys around him chuckled.

Rishikesh clenched his jaw. "Stay out of it."

"Why?" Arjun shrugged. "That day she saved you." His smile widened "Who's going to save you now?"

The words landed exactly where he intended.

He grabbed Arjun by the collar. The crowd gasped.

Arjun, however, looked almost pleased. "Careful," he whispered.

Too late.

Rishikesh's fist connected with his jaw. The corridor exploded into chaos. Students rushed forward, some tried to separate them others simply watched. Arjun stumbled back dramatically then struck back. The fight became impossible to control. Punches, shouting, furniture crashing into the wall. Everything happened in seconds. Yet through it all, Arjun seemed strangely composed, almost prepared. As though this was exactly what he wanted.

Then came the voice.

"WARDEN SIR!"

One of Arjun's friends had already sprinted down the corridor. Within moments, the hostel warden arrived. The fight stopped immediately.

Too late.

The damage had been done.

Arjun stood on one side, supported by his friends.

Rishikesh stood on the other, breathing heavily.

"What's going on here?" the warden demanded. Before Rishikesh could answer, three voices spoke at once.

"Sir, he attacked Arjun."

"Without any reason."

"We all saw it."

Rishikesh stared at them.

Every statement had been rehearsed, every witness conveniently belonged to Arjun's group. The realization hit him instantly. This had been planned, from the first insult, to the first punch, to the warden arriving at the exact moment.

Arjun lowered his eyes, pretending innocence, the perfect victim.

And Rishikesh, standing there with bruised knuckles and a shattered temper, looked exactly like the aggressor.

"I'll set up an inquiry, the decision will be made by tomorrow morning. Everyone get back to their rooms, now."

The fight left both of them severely injured. Every muscle in Rishikesh's body ached. The fight with Arjun had ended hours ago, but the pain seemed determined to linger. He lay flat on his hostel bed, staring at the ceiling fan spinning lazily above him. His knuckles were swollen, his lip was split, a dark bruise had begun forming near his ribs. Across the room, Varun arrived as soon as he heard about the fight, Rishikesh sat on a chair applying an ice pack to his own shoulder.

"You know," Varun said, wincing, "normal people celebrate relationships by going on dates."

Rishikesh groaned. "Not now."

"You, on the other hand, celebrate by getting into fights."

Rishikesh threw a pillow in his direction, but varun caught it "Bullseye."

Despite the joke, neither laughed for long, the room fell silent. Rishikesh closed his eyes, his thoughts drifted back to Aashna.

The entire night passed in discomfort. Every attempt to sleep ended with pain shooting through his body. When dawn finally arrived, he was already awake. Unfortunately, the day was about to get worse.

At around ten in the morning, an announcement echoed through the hostel corridors. All students are requested to gather in the common hall immediately, confused murmurs filled the building. Students stepped out of their rooms and made their way downstairs, rishikesh followed.

The hostel warden stood near the podium holding a file, his expression was stern. A few faculty members stood beside him, the atmosphere immediately felt wrong. The warden adjusted his spectacles. "Yesterday's violent incident in the hostel has been reviewed by the disciplinary committee." A wave of whispers spread through the crowd, Rishikesh already knew where this was heading. "The committee has decided to take strict action." The hall fell silent. "Student Rishikesh Mehra is hereby rusticated from the college for five academic days."

More whispers erupted, Rishikesh remained expressionless. Then came the second announcement. "Furthermore, due to repeated involvement in violent incidents, his hostel residency is terminated with immediate effect." The words hit harder than expected. Immediate effect. Meaning today, meaning now, meaning he had nowhere to stay.

The warden continued speaking, but Rishikesh stopped listening. His mind had already begun calculating the problem. Where would he go? How would he find accommodation? How much money would it cost?

The announcement ended, students slowly dispersed. Some offered sympathetic looks, others seemed entertained. Varun walked beside him in silence. Only after they reached the room did he speak.

"Well." Rishikesh sighed.

"Well, that could've gone better." Rishikesh laughed bitterly.

"Could've gone worse too."

"How?"

"They could've expelled me." Varun considered it.

"Fair."

The two spent the next few hours packing, the room that had once felt permanent suddenly looked temporary. Books disappeared into cartons, clothes into bags, memories into boxes.

By evening, everything was packed. Rishikesh looked around the nearly empty room, a strange sadness settled inside him. This place had witnessed years of his life, be it late-night conversations, or exam stress, Celebrations or failures. And now he was leaving it behind.

He picked up the final bag "Let's go."

Varun didn't move.

Rishikesh frowned "What?"

Varun shrugged.

"I'm coming too."

"What?"

"I'm leaving the hostel."

Rishikesh blinked "Why?"

Varun looked offended "What do you mean why?"

"Because you don't have to."

Varun zipped his backpack "Exactly."

The simplicity of the answer stunned him.

"Varun..."

"I'm not letting you live alone while you're suspended, injured and probably one inconvenience away from committing murder."

Despite himself, Rishikesh laughed.

"I'm serious."

"So am I."

Varun slung his bag over his shoulder "You're my brother, idiot."

The words landed heavily. For a moment, neither spoke, then Rishikesh quietly smiled "Thank you."

Varun immediately pointed a finger "Don't make this emotional."

"Too late."

"Disgusting."

Both laughed, And together they walked out of the hostel.

The next two days were exhausting, they visited apartment after apartment. Some landlords refused students outright, some demanded absurd deposits. Others offered rooms that looked as though they were one strong wind away from collapsing. By the second evening, frustration had reached its peak. "I'm telling you," Varun said while climbing another staircase, "at this point we should just buy a tent."

Rishikesh laughed "A luxurious downgrade."

"Exactly."

The landlord opened the door, the apartment wasn't impressive. It wasn't large, the paint was slightly faded, the furniture was old, but it was clean and more specifically affordable. And only fifteen minutes away from campus.

Rishikesh walked through the rooms, a small living area, a kitchen and a bedroom.

For the first time in days, something felt right. Varun noticed his expression "Oh no."

"What?"

"That's the face."

"What face?"

"The face people make before making bad financial decisions."

Rishikesh smiled "I think this is it."

Varun looked around once more, then nodded. "Yeah."

For once, he agreed. "I think so too."

That evening they signed the agreement.

As they carried their luggage inside, exhaustion finally gave way to relief. The apartment wasn't much, but it was theirs.

Another week passed, then another. The empty chair beside him in library remained empty, the tea stall owner had started asking where his friend was, the puppies still waited every evening near the same corner.

Aashna didn't come.

Nearly a month passed before Rishikesh finally admitted something to himself, he missed her. Not in the poetic way people wrote about in books, he missed her in ordinary moments. When he saw a novel she would've loved, when he ordered tea and instinctively asked for two cups or when he watched a sunset and reached for a hand that wasn't there.

Those moments hurt the most, because there was nothing he could do. No number to call, no address to visit, no way to reach her. Only memories, and hope, a fragile, stubborn hope that refused to die.

Every morning he still looked towards the college gate, every evening he still checked his phone, and every night he still convinced himself of the same thing.

Maybe tomorrow.

Maybe tomorrow she would come back.

CHAPTER SEVENTEEN

MRUNAL'S BIRTHDAY

More than a month had passed since Aashna's last call. The days had begun blending into one another. Rishikesh's routine had become painfully simple: wake up, attend classes, return to the apartment, stare at his phone, sleep. Repeat. The world continued moving forward, but he didn't.

One evening, Varun threw himself dramatically onto the sofa and announced, "I have officially decided that you are the most boring human being alive."

Rishikesh looked up from the book he wasn't actually reading. "Thank you."

"I'm serious. College, room, college, room, room, college. Even prisoners have a more exciting routine."

Rishikesh rolled his eyes. "Get to the point."

"The point is that we're going to Mrunal's birthday party tonight."

"We?"

"Yes, we."

"No."

Varun groaned loudly. "Brother, you're twenty-one, not eighty-one. This is the final year of our degree, have fun while you can"

"I'm not in the mood."

"You haven't been in the mood for anything for a month."

Rishikesh fell silent. Varun immediately regretted his tone.

He softened "Rishi, I know you miss her." The words hit harder than expected "But locking yourself inside isn't going to bring her back."

Rishikesh stared at the floor. For a moment he almost refused again. Then, exhausted by his own loneliness, he finally nodded."Fine."

Varun jumped from the sofa. "That's my boy."

Mrunal's house was already crowded when they arrived. Koi mil gaya songs echoed through a CD, people danced freely in the living area, laughter filled the air and colored lights flickered across smiling faces. For everyone else, it was a celebration, but for Rishikesh, it felt like he had accidentally entered somebody else's life.

Mrunal greeted them warmly. For a brief moment, genuine happiness appeared on her face upon seeing him.

"You're here."

Varun answered before Rishikesh could "After three hours of convincing."

Mrunal laughed "That sounds about right."

The evening continued. People danced, photographs were taken, cake was cut and the music grew louder. Rishikesh remained mostly quiet, standing near the balcony while others enjoyed themselves.

Then someone suggested cards, the idea was immediately accepted. Mrunal began organizing everyone while searching for a deck. "Sushmita!" she shouted over the music. "The cards are in my room. Top shelf of the cupboard." Sushmita ran upstairs.

A minute later she appeared at the doorway. "Too high!"

Mrunal laughed "I'll come."

But at that exact moment another group of guests pulled her away, the music swallowed her voice. Sushmita looked around helplessly, then spotted Rishikesh standing near the staircase.

"Rishikesh!"

He looked up.

"Can you help me get the cards?"

"Sure." He followed her upstairs.

The room was quiet compared to the chaos downstairs, sushmita pointed towards the cupboard.

"The top shelf."

Rishikesh reached up and grabbed the box of cards. As he pulled it forward, something else shifted. Three envelopes slipped from behind it, they fell to the floor. Sushmita immediately grabbed the cards "Thanks!" and disappeared downstairs.

Rishikesh bent down absentmindedly to pick up the envelopes. Then froze, the handwriting. His heart skipped a beat.

No. It couldn't be.

His eyes moved across the envelope, A name.

Aashna.

For a moment the room seemed to tilt beneath him. His breathing became shallow, the envelope trembled in his hands. There were three of them. One opened and rest two unopened. All were addressed to Mrunal and were written recently.

He opened the first letter, its envelope was already tore. His eyes rushed across the page.

"Dear Mrunal,

I hope you're doing well, I need a favour. Its been weeks since I left and I have written to Rishikesh more times than I can count, each one carefully marked to his hostel address so that it could reach him but there's no reply, not even a word.

Please ask him to contact me as soon as possible, It is very urgent.

- Aashna"

The letter slipped slightly in his hands. Received ten days ago, his heartbeat accelerated.

He immediately tore open the second envelope, this time his hands were shaking.

"Dear Mrunal,

I don't know if my words are reaching you. I have noone else to turn to.

Things are becoming complicated in my house, my cousin overheard my conversation with Rishikesh at a call and told my dad about it. Now, he is forcing me into a marriage. I love Rishikesh, I have written to him countless times but there is still no reply. I only want to know his answer.I have nowhere else to go

-Aashna"

The words blurred. Marriage, forced, countless times, no reply. Aashna had needed him, and he wasn't there. His chest tightened painfully.

Every day he had waited for her.

Every day she had waited for him.

And somehow, neither had reached the other. With trembling fingers, he opened the final envelope. A strange dread settled inside him, as though he already knew this would be the worst one.

"Dear Mrunal,

My marriage is in six days, there's no other option left. Ask Rishi one last time, If he ever loved me.. If he still cares.. Ask him to come. I will pack my luggage and wait for him. He is my only hope, I have nowhere to go except him.

If he does not come, I will understand that his love was never true.

- Aashna"

The letter ended there. No dramatic goodbye, no accusations, just surrender. The paper slipped from his fingers. Rishikesh stood motionless, unable to breathe, unable to think, unable to comprehend what he had just read.

She had waited, believed in him, trusted him, needed him. And he never came.

Not because he didn't love her, not because he abandoned her, but because he never knew. Slowly he pressed the letter against his chest. As though doing so could somehow lessen the pain, it didn't.

Footsteps echoed behind him, Mrunal entered the room. The smile on her face disappeared instantly, because she saw the letters, and she saw his expression. The silence lasted only a second.

"What are these?" His voice was low, dangerously low.

Mrunal's face turned pale. "Rishi..."

"What are these?"

She couldn't answer.

His voice rose "You knew."

Tears immediately filled her eyes "Rishi, please—"

"You knew!" The room echoed with the accusation.

"Why?" His voice cracked "Why would you do this?"

Mrunal began crying "Because I loved you." The confession landed heavily. "I thought she was the reason we could never be together"

Her words came between sobs.

"I read the first letter and she was simply asking me to tell you to contact her, I thought if you guys remained apart for some time... maybe one day...you'll move on"

Rishikesh stared at her in disbelief.

"Maybe one day, you would notice the person standing beside you all long. When the next two letters arrived I assumed it was another request to contact you" she continued with guilt appearing in her voice " So I avoided opening them"

The anger inside him transformed into something worse, disappointment.

"How can a person be so selfish" His voice was cold, sharp.

"That's not love, mrunal" he continued "That's pure selfishness."

Mrunal flinched. Each word struck harder than the last.

With shaking hands, she snatched the remaining letters from his grasp and unfolded them one by one. As her eyes moved across the pages, her breathing became uneven.

Every line carried aashna's desperation, every paragraph revealed a battle she had been fighting alone, every word exposed a pain Mrunal had chosen not to see. The letters trembled in her hands as guilt crashed over her.

"A girl was begging for help." He took the letters back from her hand. "And you hid these?"

More tears rolled down her cheeks. "I was wrong."

"Wrong?" Rishikesh laughed bitterly "She lost everything." his voice cracked "And I wasn't there when she needed me."

The guilt was unbearable, the anger even worse.

Mrunal tried to step closer.

"Rishi—"

"Don't."

The single word stopped her. For the first time since knowing him, she saw genuine hatred in his eyes.

"I will never forgive this."

The room fell silent. Then Rishikesh turned and walked away, past the music, past the laughter, past the celebration. Mrunal ran after him, calling his name, begging him to stop.

But he didn't.

The roads outside swallowed him whole, and for the first time in months, Rishikesh finally understood the truth.

CHAPTER EIGHTEEN

The Walls Closing In

The call ended.

For a few seconds, Aashna remained seated on the floor beside the window, clutching the telephone handset against her chest. Hearing Rishikesh's voice had eased some of her pain. Not all of it. Nothing could fill the void Dadujaan had left behind. But for a brief moment she had felt less alone.

"Who were you talking to?"

The voice startled her. Aashna turned abruptly, her cousin stood at the doorway. The smile immediately vanished from her face.

"No one."

He frowned. "You were crying."

Aashna quickly wiped her eyes. "It was a friend from college."

He nodded slowly, though his expression suggested he wasn't convinced. Aashna thought nothing of it. By evening, she understood her mistake. The door of her room burst open, her father stormed inside. Behind him stood her mother, terrified.

"A friend?" he shouted.

"That is what you call him?"

Aashna's heart dropped.

The cousin, he had told him. Her father threw the telephone onto the bed.

"So this is what you've been doing in the name of studies?"

Aashna lowered her gaze. "Abba—"

"Don't call me that!"

His voice shook the room, he turned toward her mother. "I told you!" His finger pointed accusingly. "I told all of you this would happen, a girl doesn't need to study in another city, a girl doesn't need to become a writer."

"Now look." His anger grew with every word "She has brought shame upon this family."

Her mother stood silently, helpless. Still mourning her father in law's death, still unable to challenge her husband.

Aashna felt tears gathering again, not because of his words but because Dadujaan was gone. Had he been alive, this conversation would never have happened.

Her father continued "The girl is getting out of hand." Then he looked at her directly "You will not step outside this room."

Aashna's chest tightened "What?"

"Lock the door." He turned toward her mother "Open it only when she needs food."

For a moment, neither woman moved then her mother quietly obeyed.

The lock clicked and Aashna was left alone.

That night felt endless, the room seemed smaller than ever. She cried until there were no tears left, not for herself but for Dadujaan, for the future slipping through her fingers, for Rishikesh and for everything.

The following days passed slowly. Painfully. The house felt different after Dadujaan's death, it felt Colder. As though the only person who had protected her dreams had been erased from existence.

One afternoon, while passing her room, she overheard her father speaking to her mother. "I've fixed the proposal." Aashna immediately moved closer to the door, Her heart pounding. "The boy is Mustafa's son." Her mother sounded uncertain "Zaid?"

"Yes."

"He's a lawyer."

"Good family, Good income." Her father sounded satisfied "The wedding will happen soon."

Aashna felt the ground disappear beneath her feet, her heart forgot to beat. How? How could she marry someone else when she loves Rishikesh.

That evening her mother entered the room carrying dinner. For a long moment neither spoke, then softly she said,

"Your father wants what is best for you."

Aashna laughed bitterly "No." her voice trembled. "He wants what's easiest, he just wants to take the burden off"

Her mother lowered her eyes "Aashna..."

"I won't marry him." The answer came immediately. Firm and certain.

"I love someone else."

Silence filled the room, her mother looked heartbroken. Not angry, just defeated. Because she already knew she could not change her husband's decision.

Two days later, desperation pushed Aashna toward the only option she had left.

Naeema.

Her childhood friend, the neighbour whose balcony stood opposite hers. Late at night, Aashna scribbled a short note, folded it carefully and turned it into a paper plane then threw it through the window. For one terrifying second, it seemed destined to fall. Instead, it landed perfectly inside Naeema's balcony.

Aashna waited.

Moments later, Naeema appeared. Confused, then concerned. After reading the note, she looked toward Aashna's window, aashna folded her hands pleadingly. Please.

Naeema hesitated, then nodded.

From that day onward, Aashna wrote letters to Rishikesh every single day. Pages filled with hope, questions, longing and fear. She addresses every envelope to his hostel trusting that somehow they would find him.

The first letter.

No reply.

The second.

Nothing.

The third.

Silence.

The fourth, the fifth, then the sixth.

Still nothing.

At first she convinced herself he was busy, then she blamed the postal service, then she blamed fate. Anything except him, because she refused to believe Rishikesh would ignore her. Yet each passing day made the silence harder to understand.

Weeks passed, the wedding discussions intensified. Relatives began visiting, jewellery appeared, fabric samples arrived, dates were discussed over cups of tea. Every conversation felt like another brick being added to a wall around her, A wall she could not escape.

Finally, with no response from Rishikesh, she turned toward her last hope.

Mrunal.

The first letter was simple.

A request, a plea to tell Rishikesh to contact her.

Days passed, nothing came, then five more days, still no reply, Her fear deepened

So she wrote again, this time explaining everything about her father, the marriage, the pressure, the desperation and how badle she wanted Rishikesh to be with her through this storm.

Again she waited, again silence answered.

By now wedding preparations had begun in earnest. Relatives filled the house, invitations were discussed, gold jewellery was purchased. And every night Aashna lay awake wondering whether Rishikesh had forgotten her or whether something had happened to him.

Then, with trembling hands, she wrote one final letter. The hardest letter she had ever written.

"Dear Mrunal,

My marriage is in four days, there's no other option left. Ask Rishi one last time, If he ever loved me.. If he still cares.. Ask him to come. I will pack my luggage and wait for him. He is my only hope, I have nowhere to go except him.

If he does not come, I will understand that his love was never true.

- Aashna"

When she finished writing, a tear fell onto the paper. Aashna wiped it away, folded the letter and handed it to Naeema the following morning through her room window.

Then she waited.

For a reply.

For a miracle.

For Rishikesh.

CHAPTER NINETEEN

TOO LATE?

The night refused to end.

Rishikesh left Mrunal's house without knowing where his feet were taking him. The city lights blurred through the tears he refused to wipe. Aashna's letters remained crushed in his hand, their edges damp from the sweat of his trembling palms.

He had read them again on the road.

Then again.

As if the words might change the fourth time.

They never did.

My marriage is in six days. The sentence kept echoing inside his head like a cruel prayer.

By the time he reached the bus stand, it was past midnight. The place was crowded with travelers wrapped in shawls, vendors pouring tea into small paper cups, and buses arriving with loud engines and tired headlights. Rishikesh stood beneath a flickering tube light clutching his backpack, feeling as though the entire world was moving while his own life had stopped.

The next bus to Srinagar was delayed.

Three hours.

Three unbearable hours.

He sat on a cold metal bench and stared at the road ahead. Every few minutes he checked the letters again, as though afraid they would disappear too. Guilt gnawed at him relentlessly. Aashna had waited for him. She had trusted him. She had believed he would come.

And he had not.

Not because he didn't love her.

Because he never knew.

The realization was suffocating.

When the bus finally arrived near dawn, Rishikesh boarded it in silence. He took the window seat and rested his head against the glass as the city slowly disappeared behind him. The journey felt endless. Mountains rose in the distance, rivers flashed past, villages blurred into one another, but he saw none of it clearly. His mind kept returning to Aashna.

Was she married already?

Was she still waiting?

Had she cried thinking he abandoned her?

At one point he took out the last letter again. His fingers traced her handwriting gently, almost reverently.

He is my only hope.Rishikesh shut his eyes.

"I'm coming, Aashi," he whispered into the darkness of the moving bus. "Please... just hold on."

Morning arrived pale and cold over Srinagar. The bus stopped near the terminal, and Rishikesh stepped out with stiff legs and a pounding heart. Without wasting a moment, he hired a taxi and showed the driver the address written on Aashna's envelope.

"Aragam?" the driver asked.

Rishikesh nodded.

The journey through Kashmir was breathtaking, but beauty had become meaningless to him. Snow-touched mountains stood silently in the distance, and the Jhelum flowed calmly beside the road, indifferent to the storm inside him. Four hours passed in restless silence.

Then the taxi turned into a narrow lane lined with old houses and chinar trees.

"Yahi hoga," the driver said softly.

Rishikesh stepped out.

His heartbeat thundered in his ears.

At the end of the lane stood a house decorated with fading wedding flowers and strings of lights. Some decorations still hung loosely from the gate, swaying in the cold breeze.

For a moment, he couldn't move.

The sight alone told him the truth his heart had been refusing to accept.

This house had been decorated for her wedding.

For making Aashna someone else's.

He walked toward it slowly, each step heavier than the last. The gate was locked. The courtyard stood empty. A few men nearby were removing the remaining decorations and loading them into a truck.

Rishikesh approached one of them. "Brother, is the wedding over?"

The man glanced at him casually while pulling down a garland. "Yes.. two days ago."

Two days ago. The words struck him like a blow to the chest. For a second, the world tilted, he gripped the gate to steady himself. His eyes burned, but he forced himself not to break down there in front of strangers.

"Do you know... where the bride was married?" he asked, his voice barely holding together.

The man shook his head. "Pata nahi bhai. Shayad kisi aur town mein. Baraat bahar se aayi thi."

Rishikesh nodded mechanically. "Thank you."

He turned away before the man could see the tears gathering in his eyes. The lane blurred before him. The taxi driver called after him, asking whether he wanted to go somewhere else, but Rishikesh kept standing as he didn't know where to go anymore.

Rishikesh stood there, stunned- his eyes fixed on the house as if willing her to appear, to come and hold him around her arms just as fiercely, her fingers trembling at his back, whispering "I knew you'd come." He closed his eyes, letting the illusion warm him for a second, But when opened them.. there was no one. His chest ached with the weight of her absence- his arms still waiting for the hug that didn't happen.

She was gone, and now she belonged to a life that didn't include him. She had waited but he came too late.

A few minutes later, he reached the side of a quiet road near the fields outside the village. There was no one there. Only the cold wind and the distant sound of a river. And there, finally, he broke.

He sank onto the ground beside the road, clutching Aashna's letters against his chest. A sob escaped him before he could stop it, then another, until the grief he had been holding back all night poured out uncontrollably.

"Why?" he whispered hoarsely into the empty air.

He laughed bitterly through tears. "You said destiny would bring us together."

The mountains remained silent, the wind carried away his words. Rishikesh lowered his head into his hands and cried like a man mourning not just a person, but an entire future. Because somewhere between the library cupboard, the rain, the sunflowers, and the letters that never reached him...

He had already built a life with Aashna in his heart.

And now, sitting alone on a cold Kashmiri roadside, he believed he had lost it forever.

CHAPTER TWENTY

BRIDE WHO WAITED

Six days.

That was all that remained.

Six days between Aashna and a future she never wanted.

The house had transformed into a place she no longer recognized. Every morning new relatives arrived. Every evening more wedding preparations were discussed. Voices echoed through the hallways, laughter filled the courtyard, and the sound of dholki seemed to follow her wherever she went.

Everyone was happy, everyone except the bride.

Aashna sat by the window of her room, staring at the road beyond the gate, waiting. It had become a habit now. every passing vehicle made her heart race, every unfamiliar voice made her look up, every knock on the gate forced hope into her chest. Maybe it was him, maybe Rishikesh had finally received her letters, maybe he was coming but the gate remained empty. Always empty.

At night she would replay every memory of him in her mind. The library, the sticky notes, the rainy afternoon, the tea stall, the confession at Triveni Ghat, the way he used to look at her as though she was the most precious thing he had ever found.

She refused to believe that man had forgotten her. Something had happened, something had to have happened. Otherwise he would have come, he would have replied, he would have fought the entire world for her. She knew he would.

Yet each passing day made that belief harder to hold onto.

The wedding preparations only intensified. Soon the house was overflowing with guests, aunts she barely remembered, cousins she hadn't seen in years, children running through the hallways. Everyone discussing jewelry, clothes, decorations and the groom.

The groom, the word itself made her sick.

The Mehendi ceremony arrived.

The courtyard glowed beneath strings of golden lights. Women sat together singing traditional songs while others beat the dholki rhythmically. Laughter echoed everywhere.

Aashna sat in the center wearing a green suit chosen by her mother. She felt like a spectator in her own life.

The mehendi artist smiled warmly. "Such beautiful hands." Aashna forced a smile. The intricate designs slowly spread across her palms and wrists. Everyone admired them, her cousins teased her endlessly. Someone mentioned Zaid, someone joked about her future, someone asked if she was nervous.

Aashna answered nothing.

She simply stared at the entrance gate. Waiting, still waiting. As though Rishikesh might appear at any moment and he would somehow stop all of this.

Hours later the design was completed, the artist admired her work proudly "There."

Everyone gathered around excitedly, one of her cousins gasped. "Show us where his name is hidden!" The artist laughed and pointed toward the center of her palm.

Aashna lowered her gaze.

And froze.

There it was, written elegantly within the design.

Zaid.

The world suddenly became quiet, the songs disappeared, the laughter disappeared, everything disappeared, Only the name remained.

Zaid.

Not Rishikesh.

Not the man she loved, not the man she had chosen. A sharp pain rose in her chest and her breathing became uneven. The courtyard seemed to spin around her, someone asked if she was alright, another cousin laughed, assuming she was simply shy.

But Aashna could barely hear them, her heart was pounding uncontrollably. Tears gathered in her eyes, then she stood abruptly. Without saying a word, she turned and hurried inside. The voices behind her faded, she reached her room and slammed the door shut. Her chest rose and fell rapidly.

No.

No.

No.

Her eyes remained fixed on the name.

Zaid.

It felt wrong.

Like a stain, like an insult to everything she and Rishikesh had shared. Tears streamed down her cheeks. She rushed to the washbasin and opened the tap. Water flowed endlessly over her hands, she rubbed frantically again and again.

The mehendi lightened slightly but refused to disappear, the name remained mocking her.

Aashna's panic deepened and her breathing became erratic, she scrubbed harder.

Still there.

Then her eyes landed on a steel scrubber lying near the sink. Without thinking, she grabbed it and started rubbing. The rough metal scraped against her skin, pain shot through her hand but she didn't stop.

The design blurred and her skin reddened. Still she continued. The scrubber tore against her flesh. The burning became unbearable. Yet she kept going, as though removing the name would somehow stop the marriage itself, as though erasing Zaid would bring Rishikesh back.

"Aashna!"

The voice startled her.

Her mother stood frozen at the doorway, horror spread across her face.

The steel scrubber slipped from Aashna's hand, blood mixed with water in the basin.

Her mother's eyes widened, she immediately rushed forward and closed the room door behind her.

"What are you doing?" she cried "Have you lost your mind?"

Aashna looked down at her bleeding hand, then at the fading name. A fresh wave of tears escaped her.

"I can't do this." Her voice broke "I can't."

Her mother grabbed her shoulders. "Aashna..."

"I belong to Rishikesh." the words came out through sobs. "I belong to him and only him."

The room fell silent, for a moment even her mother couldn't speak. She simply looked at her daughter, broken, terrified and desperate.

A girl who was being dragged toward a life she did not want. Tears filled her mother's eyes too, but unlike Aashna, she had long ago learned what it meant to surrender.

She joined her hands, actually folded them before her own daughter. The sight shattered Aashna.

"Please," her mother whispered "Please don't do this." another tear slipped down her cheek. "I know you're hurting, I know."

"But I cannot fight him." Her voice trembled. "Come outside Aashna, please."

The plea wasn't coming from a mother enforcing rules, It was coming from a helpless woman trapped by the same system that had now trapped her daughter. For several moments neither moved. Then slowly, painfully, Aashna nodded. Her mother carefully cleaned the wounds on her hand, covered them with a cloth and led her back toward the courtyard.

The music was still playing, the guests were still laughing, the celebration continued as though nothing had happened. And Aashna returned to the center of it all, carrying a smile she did not feel and a heart that was quietly breaking with every passing day.

Two days remained.

Only two.

The realization haunted Aashna every waking moment.

The house had become busier than ever. Relatives occupied every room, children ran through the corridors, women discussed wedding preparations endlessly, and guests continued arriving from distant towns. Amidst all the noise, Aashna carried a secret.

A suitcase.

Hidden beneath her bed.

Every night, after everyone had fallen asleep, she quietly pulled it out and added something to it. A pair of clothes, her notebooks, the poems she had written over the years, a photograph of Dadujaan.

The suitcase wasn't large, it didn't need to be, it only contained the pieces of a life she hoped to carry with her because somewhere deep inside, she still believed he would come.

She had planned everything, the back gate remained unlocked after midnight. The road behind the orchard connected directly to the main highway. All she needed was Rishikesh, just him, just once, just one glimpse of him standing outside the gate then she would leave everything behind without looking back.

For a moment, a dangerous thought crossed her mind.

What if she escaped alone? What if she boarded a bus and searched for him herself?

The thought lingered, tempting, desperate.

Then fear followed.

What if he had already received the letters?

What if he had chosen silence?

What if he didn't want the responsibility that came with loving someone?

What if she arrived at his doorstep and found disappointment waiting instead?

What if he opened the door and looked at her with unfamiliar eyes?

What if he said no?

The questions suffocated her.

If that happened, where would she go and who would she turn to?

The world was not kind to women who ran away from home. Especially not women from families like hers.

Aashna hugged her knees tightly and sat beside the suitcase for a long time, then she wiped her tears.

No. She knew Rishikesh. The man who waited for her outside libraries, the man who hated rain but stood soaking wet beside her at the tea stall, the man who had promised to protect her dreams, the man who had looked at her as though she was his entire world.

If he knew... he would come, he would fight for her, he would make her his. The certainty soothed her heart and so the suitcase remained packed,waiting, just like her.

The wedding day arrived.

Aashna had not slept, not even for a moment. Every hour of the night had been spent staring at the window, listening, waiting and praying.

When dawn broke, her cousins flooded into the room. The day had begun. The bride needed to be prepared, Aashna sat silently while they fussed around her, someone braided her hair, someone selected jewelry, someone joked about married life, someone teased her endlessly.

She heard none of it.

Every few minutes her eyes drifted toward the window. The gate remained visible from there, still no sign of him. Morning passed, the sun climbed higher.

Still nothing.

Afternoon arrived, guests continued filling the house. The cars were parked outside and laughter echoed from every corner.

Still nothing.

Aashna checked the gate again.

And again.

And again.

Nothing.

By evening, hope had begun to hurt. The bridal room fell silent as the final touches were completed. Aashna stood before the mirror, for a moment she failed to recognize herself. The red bridal joda shimmered beneath the lights, golden embroidery flowed across the fabric and heavy jewelry rested around her neck. The dupatta framed her face perfectly, anyone looking at her would have called her beautiful, not only beautiful but majestic, radiant.

But Aashna couldn't bear her own reflection because this wasn't how she had imagined it. This wasn't supposed to happen, not like this, not with someone else.

Every dream she had ever built around marriage had included only one face; Rishikesh.

Only him.

A tear threatened to escape, she quickly wiped it before it ruined her makeup.

Outside, sudden noise erupted, the baraat had arrived. The sound of drums echoed through the house, cheers followed. Relatives hurried toward the entrance.

The groom had come.

Just not the one she wanted.

Aashna lowered her gaze. For the first time, fear outweighed hope. What if he truly wasn't coming? Some time later, the door opened. Her mother entered quietly.

"Aashna." Her voice was gentle. "It's time."

The words shattered something inside her. She stood on trembling legs, the walk toward the ceremony felt endless. Each step heavier than the last, each breath more difficult than the one before. When they finally reached the gathering, all eyes turned toward her.

The bride.

Aashna sat down.

Her hands felt cold, her heartbeat was deafening. Across from her sat Zaid, a stranger, a man she barely knew.

The Qazi began the formalities, the room fell silent.

Then came the question.

"Zaid sahab, aapko Aashna se nikah qubool hai?"

Without hesitation, he replied.

"Qubool hai."

The Qazi repeated it.

Again. "Qubool hai."

A third time. "Qubool hai."

Each answer came effortlessly and confidently. As though this was exactly what he wanted.

Then the Qazi turned toward her, his voice was calm.

"Beti, aapko Zaid se nikah qubool hai?"

Aashna froze. The world stopped, she couldn't breathe, she couldn't speak, she couldn't hear anything except the pounding of her own heart.

The silence stretched.

The Qazi repeated the question. "Beti, aapko Zaid se nikah qubool hai?"

Still nothing. Around her, murmurs began spreading. Relatives exchanged confused glances, someone whispered, someone shifted uneasily.

Aashna stared at the floor, waiting, one final time. For a miracle, for footsteps, for a familiar voice calling her name.

Nothing came.

Her father shot a warning glance toward her mother, a deadly one, the kind that needed no words.

Her mother gently placed a hand on her shoulder. Aashna looked up. Her mother's eyes were filled with helplessness and pain.

"Aashna," she whispered softly. "Qubool hai beta."

A tear slid down Aashna's cheek, slowly she closed her eyes. And there he was, Rishikesh. Standing beneath the rain, smiling at her, holding her hand, waiting for her, looking at her through his innocent eyes, as though she was poetry itself.

For one final moment she held onto that image, then reality tore it away. Her lips trembled, another tear escaped. And finally, in a voice barely louder than a whisper, she said—

"Qubool hai."
The words left her mouth.
And with them, the future she had once dreamed of.

CHAPTER TWENTY-ONE

The Man Left Behind

The journey back to Rishikesh felt longer than the one to Kashmir.

When he had left, hope had accompanied him.

Now he returned alone.

The bus window reflected a face he barely recognized. His eyes were swollen from crying, dark circles resting beneath them. His beard had begun growing unevenly, and exhaustion seemed etched into every feature. Around him, passengers chatted, slept, argued over seats, and complained about the weather.

Life continued.

His did not.

Throughout the journey, Aashna's final letter remained folded inside his jacket pocket.

He must have read it a hundred times.

Each time the same sentence shattered him.

"If he ever loved me, ask him to come."

He had come. Just two days too late.

Two days, such a small amount of time. Yet enough to destroy an entire future.

When the bus finally reached Rishikesh, evening had begun settling over the city. The familiar streets felt strangely foreign. He walked toward the apartment he shared with Varun, dragging his bag behind him.

His body was tired, his soul was exhausted. The apartment door opened before he could knock. Varun stood there holding a cup of tea, the smile on his face disappeared immediately. For a moment he simply stared. Rishikesh looked as though he had aged years in a matter of days, his clothes were wrinkled, his eyes were empty and there was a silence around him that frightened Varun.

"Rishi?"

No response.

"Brother, what happened?"

The bag slipped from Rishikesh's hand, he looked at Varun. For several seconds, he tried to speak but nothing came out. Then finally, his voice cracked.

"Aashna got married."

The words barely left his mouth before everything collapsed. Months of fear, days of hope, hours of desperate travel. All of it shattered at once.

Rishikesh sank onto the floor his shoulders trembled violently. Varun had never seen him cry like that, not after fights, not after failures, not after any setback life had thrown at him.

This was different, this was grief, the kind that hollowed a person from the inside. Varun quietly sat beside him, no advice, no motivational speeches, no false promises, just silent companionship.

Because some wounds were too deep for words.

The days that followed became difficult to remember not because anything remarkable happened, because nothing did. Rishikesh attended classes, submitted assignments, prepared for examinations, ate when reminded, slept when exhaustion forced him to.

He functioned but he no longer lived.

The world around him gradually faded into the background, his laughter disappeared first, then his enthusiasm, then his desires.

Every place carried her memory, the library reminded him of sticky notes hidden inside books, the tea stall reminded him of rain-soaked afternoons, the campus grounds reminded him of her laughter. Even sunsets became unbearable.

Everything in his life belonged to her, everything.

Some evenings he would walk aimlessly along the ghats for hours watching the Ganga flow endlessly before him, sometimes he sat on the same steps until midnight, staring into the dark water without thinking about anything at all.

Other times he thought about everything. What if he had checked the hostel letterbox earlier? What if he had found the letters sooner? What if he had reached Kashmir one day earlier? One hour earlier?

The questions haunted him relentlessly, and none had answers.

Varun tried, god knew he tried. He dragged him to movies, forced him to attend gatherings, invited him for cricket matches, even brought books hoping they would distract him.

Nothing worked.

The Rishikesh he knew seemed to have vanished somewhere in Kashmir, only a shadow had returned.

Months passed, then more months.

Winter arrived and left.

Spring followed but still nothing changed.

Nearly a year slipped away.

Yet the pain remained fresh. As if the wedding had happened yesterday.

One evening, Varun returned to the apartment carrying a stack of notes. He dropped them dramatically onto the table. The sound finally pulled Rishikesh's attention away from the notebook lying open before him.

"What?"

Varun folded his arms.

"We are graduating in two months."

Rishikesh nodded absentmindedly. "So?"

"So?" Varun repeated in disbelief. "That is your reaction?"

"What else should it be?"

Varun rubbed his forehead, sometimes he genuinely wanted to throw a pillow at him. Instead, he took a deep breath.

"Listen carefully."

Rishikesh raised an eyebrow.

"After graduation, you're coming with me."

"Where?"

"My hometown."

"No."

Varun expected that answer. "You haven't even heard where."

"Still no."

"Bhaderwah."

"No."

"Beautiful mountains."

"No."

"Fresh air."

"No."

"Good food."

"No."

Varun groaned.

"Will you let me finish?"

Rishikesh returned to his notebook. "I'm not interested."

Varun walked over and shut it immediately.

Rishikesh looked up, annoyed.

Varun looked directly into his eyes. For once, there was no joking, no sarcasm, no laughter. Only concern.

"Brother, you're disappearing."

The words hung heavily between them.

"You sit alone, eat alone, think alone and suffer alone." Varun's voice softened. "And I can't watch it anymore."

Rishikesh looked away because deep down, he knew his friend was right.

"I'm fine."

"No, you're not."

The answer came immediately.

The silence that followed said everything.

Finally Varun sighed "Two months." He pointed a finger.

"We graduate, pack our bags, and you're coming with me."

"No excuses."

Rishikesh opened his mouth to protest.

Varun raised a hand. "Rejected."

"I'm serious."

"So am I."

For the first time in months, a faint smile almost appeared on Rishikesh's face, almost.

Varun noticed, and seized the opportunity.

"See? progress."

Rishikesh rolled his eyes, but said nothing.

Two months passed.

The final examinations arrived.

Then ended.

College life slowly came to a close. Students celebrated, photographs were taken, farewells were exchanged, promises were made. The future waited ahead for everyone. Including Rishikesh, though he wasn't sure he wanted one.

On the evening after graduation, Varun entered the apartment carrying two bags. One belonged to him, the other belonged to Rishikesh. Already packed.

Rishikesh stared at it, then at Varun.

"You packed my clothes?"

"Yes."

"You are impossible."

"I know." Varun grinned then tossed him the bag. "Come on."

"Bhaderwah awaits."

For the first time in over a year, Rishikesh stepped forward without knowing where life was taking him.

CHAPTER TWENTY-TWO

BHADERWAH

The bus departed shortly after sunset.

Varun had been unusually cheerful throughout the evening, almost as if he had personally succeeded in dragging Rishikesh away from his misery. He spent the first hour talking endlessly about Bhaderwah, describing its mountains, forests, rivers, and food with the excitement of someone introducing his favorite person to his favorite place.

Rishikesh listened quietly or at least pretended to.

The truth was that his mind was elsewhere. It always was.

By midnight, the bus had fallen silent. Most passengers had drifted into sleep. Even Varun, who had promised to keep him company throughout the journey, was now fast asleep with his head tilted awkwardly against the window.

Outside, darkness swallowed the roads.

Inside, memories refused to leave.

Rishikesh rested his forehead against the cold glass and stared at the passing silhouettes of mountains. He tried closing his eyes and immediately she appeared. Aashna, laughing without restraint, the way she would tilt her head while teasing him, the way she would pull his cheek whenever he acted too serious, the way her eyes sparkled whenever she talked about books. For a brief moment, the memory felt real enough to touch, then reality returned.

His eyes opened again. A tear escaped despite his efforts, he wiped it away before anyone could see. Sleep never came. Not that night, not for a very long time.

Morning sunlight slowly spread across the mountains as the bus entered Bhaderwah.

The valley looked almost unreal. Pine-covered hills stretched endlessly into the distance. Small houses stood peacefully among the greenery while mist floated lazily above the slopes. The air itself felt different. Cleaner and lighter. As though the mountains carried none of the burdens of the outside world.

Varun stretched dramatically before pointing outside. "There."

Rishikesh followed his gaze.

"My kingdom."

For the first time in days, a faint smile appeared on his face. "A kingdom with one bus stand?"

"Respect your king."

Varun's family welcomed him with surprising warmth.

His mother insisted on preparing breakfast immediately. His father refused to let him carry his own luggage. His younger sister bombarded him with questions before he had even settled down.

For a family meeting him for the first time, they treated him as though he had always belonged there. Yet Rishikesh found himself unable to respond properly. Every smile felt forced, every conversation required effort, love was being offered freely. But somewhere along the way he had forgotten how to receive it.

Varun noticed, he always did.

But for once he said nothing.

The following days passed quietly. Varun seemed determined to show him every corner of Bhaderwah. One morning they visited his old school. The building looked ordinary, yet Varun narrated stories from every classroom as though describing historical monuments.

"That window?" he said proudly. "I jumped out of it once."

"Why?"

"Math exam."

Rishikesh laughed despite himself. "You're an idiot."

"I know."

Another day they climbed to a viewpoint overlooking the valley. Mountains surrounded them from every direction while clouds drifted beneath the peaks. Most people would have found the view breathtaking.

Rishikesh merely nodded. "It's beautiful."

Varun looked at him suspiciously. "That's it?"

"What else?"

"Normal people cry seeing this."

"I already used up my tears."

The joke landed poorly, Varun fell silent.

On the fourth day, while sitting beside a small stream, Rishikesh finally spoke.

"I'll leave in two days."

Varun skipped a stone across the water. "Why?"

"My mother is waiting." The answer came softly. "I haven't been home in almost a year."

For a moment, neither spoke.

Then Varun nodded. "Fair enough."

Rishikesh looked toward the flowing water. His life had remained frozen while time continued moving forward, perhaps it was time to go home, perhaps it was time to stop running. Even if nothing inside him had healed.

That evening, unable to sit indoors any longer, Rishikesh decided to take a walk alone.

The trail eventually led him toward Seoj Meadow.

The valley stretched endlessly before him, covered in green grass and framed by towering coniferous trees. The setting sun painted the landscape in shades of gold and orange while the distant mountains stood silently against the horizon.

It was beautiful, painfully beautiful. The kind of place Aashna would have loved, the thought arrived automatically as every thought eventually did. He imagined her running through the meadow, collecting wildflowers, insisting on taking photographs, mocking him for being too serious.

A small smile appeared on his face, then disappeared.

Because she wasn't there, and never would be.

The realization still hurt.

The evening gradually darkened. Rishikesh finally turned around and began walking back toward town. Lost in thought, lost in memory.

Then suddenly— He stopped.

A few meters ahead, among the small crowd moving along the road, stood a familiar figure.

His heartbeat stumbled.

No.

It couldn't be.

For a moment he convinced himself he was imagining things again. The woman stood partially turned away from him. A light shawl covered her shoulders, dark hair fell softly around her face, something about her posture, something about the way she stood, something felt impossibly familiar.

Rishikesh's breathing quickened.

The crowd shifted.

The woman turned slightly.

And his world stopped.

Aashna.

His heart slammed against his ribs.

The same eyes, the same face, slightly thinner, slightly older. Her hair were tied in a loose bun.

But undeniably her.

For a second he forgot how to breathe. Then his gaze dropped lower, and froze.

A gentle curve beneath her clothes, a baby bump, pregnant?

His mind refused to process what he was seeing. Maybe he was mistaken, maybe it was just loose fabric, maybe grief had finally driven him insane. But every instinct inside him screamed otherwise.

Without thinking, he began walking faster, then faster, almost running.

"Aashna..."

The name barely escaped his lips. The crowd moved between them. A vehicle passed and before he could reach her, an auto-rickshaw stopped beside her and she stepped inside.

Rishikesh broke into a run.

"Aashna!"

The auto pulled away, Panic surged through him. Another auto stood nearby, he jumped inside immediately. "Follow that one!"

The driver looked confused."What?"

"Just follow it!"

The auto sped forward. Rishikesh's eyes never left the vehicle ahead, his pulse thundered in his ears, questions exploded inside his mind. How was she here? Why Bhaderwah? Was she happy? Did she ever think about him?

The auto eventually stopped near a residential area. Rishikesh threw money at the driver and hurried out.

The other auto stood there but Aashna.. she was gone. Completely gone.

He searched every lane, every corner.

Nothing.

As though she had vanished into thin air, the same way she had vanished from his life. Nearly an hour later, exhausted and frustrated, he returned to Varun's house.

Varun immediately noticed his expression. "What happened?"

Rishikesh sat down heavily. His voice shook"I saw her."

Varun frowned. "Saw who?"

"Aashna."

The room fell silent. Varun stared at him.

"What?"

"I saw Aashna."

He repeated firmly. "Here? In Bhaderwah?."

Varun looked uncertain. "Rishi..."

"It was her."

"You sure?"

"I'm sure."

Varun hesitated then asked carefully, "Could it be someone else?"

The question irritated him immediately. "My eyes can forget my own reflection, but they cannot forget her." The certainty in his words silenced the room.

Rishikesh looked toward the dark window. Somewhere out there, in the same town, Aashna existed. Not as a memory, not as a dream, not as a photograph but real.

And for the first time in more than a year, hope returned.

Terrifying, fragile and Impossible hope.

CHAPTER TWENTY-THREE

ONE LAST TIME

Rishikesh returned to the same lane the next morning.

Earlier than necessary.

Hope had not allowed him to sleep.

The entire night had been spent staring at the ceiling, replaying the glimpse he had caught of her in Bhaderwah. Every time he closed his eyes, he saw her standing there. Real. Alive. Not a memory. Not a dream.

Aashna.

He reached the house shortly after sunrise and stood across the road, pretending to look occupied whenever someone passed by. An hour passed. Then another. The valley slowly awakened around him. Shopkeepers opened their shutters, children walked toward schools, and distant voices echoed through the narrow streets.

Still no sign of her.

By the time the second hour ended, doubt had begun creeping into his mind. Maybe Varun had been right, maybe he had mistaken someone else for her, maybe grief had played another cruel trick.

Then the front door opened. A man stepped out, tall, well dressed, clean shaven. A black coat rested over his shoulders, a lawyer. He adjusted his watch, exchanged a few words with someone inside, and walked toward a waiting car.

The driver started the engine. As the vehicle began moving, a curtain on the first-floor window shifted slightly.

Rishikesh froze.

There she was.

Aashna.

Standing behind the glass watching the car leave. Expressionless, no smile, no warmth, nothing. Only exhaustion.

The curtain fell back into place, the car disappeared.

And for the first time in over a year, certainty settled inside him.

It was her.

He crossed the road immediately. His heartbeat pounded violently against his chest as he climbed the stairs and stopped before the door.

Then knocked.

No answer.

He knocked again.

A few seconds later, footsteps approached. The door opened, and time stopped.

Aashna stood before him.

Her hair was tied loosely into a bun. A few strands had escaped and framed her tired face. Dark circles rested beneath her eyes. She looked thinner than he remembered.

Fragile, as though life had slowly been draining her piece by piece.

For several seconds neither spoke, shock filled her eyes, pure disbelief. As though she had seen a ghost. Then suddenly she stepped back and slammed the door shut.

Rishikesh stared at the closed door.

"Aashna."

Silence.

He knocked again, no response.

"Aashna, please."

Nothing.

He continued knocking, patiently, desperately. Finally, after several minutes, the lock clicked. The door opened once more, this time she stepped aside silently.

Rishikesh entered.

The moment he was inside, she closed the door behind him. The room felt suffocatingly quiet. Aashna stood several feet away from him, keeping her distance.

"Why are you here?" she asked.

Her voice was cold, too cold. The kind of cold created by heartbreak.

Rishikesh opened his mouth but she didn't let him speak.

"What's the point of coming now?" her voice trembled despite her efforts "What's even left now?"

Her eyes glistened "You never loved me, Rishi."

The accusation landed harder than any punch he had ever received. Because he knew why she believed it. He knew what she had suffered, a tear escaped her eye, then another.

Rishikesh took a slow breath. "Aashna."

"No." She shook her head immediately "I waited." The words broke apart "I waited for you."

Rishikesh remained silent, letting her speak.

"I wrote letters."

"I begged."

"I prayed."

"I waited every day."

Her voice rose.

"And you never came."

The room fell silent.

Then Rishikesh stepped forward carefully "Listen to me."

She looked away.

"For once."

Something in his voice made her stop. "Fine." The word came reluctantly. "Speak."

And so he told her everything.

The fight, the hostel expulsion, leaving the hostel, finding a new apartment, never receiving her letters, then discovering the truth through Mrunal.

Every detail, every moment, every mistake, every second of guilt.

Aashna listened without interruption her expression gradually changed. Anger giving way to confusion, confusion giving way to heartbreak.

By the time he finished, tears were streaming freely down her face.

"It doesn't matter anymore." her voice was barely audible "It doesn't change anything."

She wiped her eyes "Just leave."

Rishikesh stared at her then nodded slowly "Fine."

The answer surprised her.

"I'll leave."

He took another step forward "But answer one question first."

She remained silent.

Rishikesh's eyes locked onto hers.

"Look into my eyes and tell me you love your husband."

The room froze.

"Tell me that." His voice cracked. "And I'll leave."

Aashna's lips trembled, The answer refused to come. Seconds passed, then tears rolled down her cheeks.

"I can't." Her voice broke completely. "I can never love someone else."

Rishikesh closed his eyes, relief and pain struck him simultaneously.

Aashna continued speaking "I only loved you." A sob escaped her "I waited for you till my wedding day." Her shoulders shook "I packed my luggage, I was ready to leave everything behind." Another tear slid down her face "But you didn't come."

Rishikesh stepped closer, this time there was no distance between them.

"I did." His voice was barely a whisper "I came, Aashi."

His hand gently wiped her tears "I was just two days late."

The sentence shattered both of them, for a moment neither could speak. The weight of lost time hung heavily between them.

Then Rishikesh's gaze slowly drifted downward, toward the gentle curve beneath her clothes.

The baby.

Questions immediately flooded his mind.

Aashna noticed, and lowered her eyes.

"You deserve to know."

The room grew quiet again. For several moments she struggled to continue, then finally she spoke.

"I didn't let him touch me." Her voice trembled. "For months."

Rishikesh listened silently.

"I couldn't." Aashna swallowed hard "I couldn't give someone else what belonged to you." Fresh tears escaped. "Then one night..." Her hands began shaking. "He came home drunk." Rishikesh's chest tightened. "I was asleep." She looked away, unable to meet his eyes. "And before I could understand what was happening..."

"Stop" Rishikesh said, as a tear rolled down his cheek. The realization hit him like a truck, his fists clenched instantly, every muscle in his body tensed. A dangerous rage surfaced.

"I'll sue him." The words came out through gritted teeth.

Aashna laughed bitterly through tears "I tried."

Rishikesh looked at her.

"I tried filing a complaint." Her voice carried defeat "The officer was his friend." She looked toward the floor. "He's a respected lawyer." A pause "And legally my husband." The bitterness in her voice was unbearable "He made consent sound ridiculous."

Silence filled the room.

"I could spend my entire life beside you, Aashna." his voice trembled. "I could love you from a distance if that's what you needed. I could sit next to you for years without touching you, if you didn't want me to."

Tears blurred her vision

Rishikesh swallowed hard, "But he... He stole from you what should have been yours to give." he felt sick, disgusted, helpless.

"Such an insult to humanity." His voice was barely audible.

Aashna simply looked away, tired, defeated, broken.

Then suddenly Rishikesh dropped to his knees in front of her, taking her trembling hand in his, eyes filled with desperation.

"Aashna." She looked down at him "Please come with me." The plea cracked his voice. "We can still have the life we dreamed of."

Aashna closed her eyes "No."

"We can."

"I can't."

"You can."

A tear slipped down her cheek. She placed a trembling hand over her stomach. "I'm carrying someone else's child." The words broke her.

Rishikesh immediately shook his head. "I don't care." Aashna stared at him. "I'll love the baby as my own." His voice never wavered. "I'll raise the child, I'll protect both of you and I'll love you exactly the same." The certainty in his eyes nearly destroyed her resolve.

Aashna slowly lowered herself before him, her trembling hands reached for his face. For the first time since he arrived, she touched him. Gently, as though afraid he might disappear. Her fingers traced his cheek, memorizing him. The man she had loved for years.

Then she leaned forward and pressed a soft kiss against his forehead. Tender, heartbreaking, full of everything words could never express.

Their foreheads rested together for a second longer, as if they were living decades in this moment. Neither wanted the moment to end, but eventually it had to.

Aashna pulled away first because she knew if she didn't, she would surrender. And if she surrendered, she would leave with him which she didn't want because she thought his life would be ruined if he married a pregnant lady, people would laugh at him.

She loved him enough to let him go. So, she looked into his eyes one last time. Then whispered softly,

"If you ever loved me..." her voice cracked. "I beg you."

A tear rolled down her face "Go away."

CHAPTER TWENTY-FOUR

A LIFE FOR A LIFE

Rishikesh descended the stairs slowly, each step feeling heavier than the last. The conversation with Aashna replayed endlessly in his mind. Her trembling voice. The tears in her eyes. The way she had begged him to leave.

If you ever loved me, I beg you to go away.

The words refused to leave him.

He wiped his eyes roughly and stepped onto the street. The cold evening air struck his face, but it did little to clear the storm raging inside him. He walked a few steps away from the house before stopping. Something felt wrong, terribly wrong.

His chest tightened. How could he leave her like that? After finding her again, after learning everything she had endured, after finally reaching her.

How could he simply walk away?

Rishikesh stood frozen for a moment before turning around. Then he ran, the stairs disappeared beneath his feet as he rushed back to her apartment. He knocked once.

No answer.

Twice, still nothing.

A sudden fear gripped him.

"Aashna!" He pushed the door open.

The sight before him drained the color from his face. Aashna was lying unconscious on the floor. "Aashna!" He rushed to her side and dropped to his knees, his hands shook violently as he lifted her head into his lap. "Aashna, wake up." but no response.

He rushed to the kitchen, grabbed water, and sprinkled it over her face.

Nothing.

Panic consumed him. For a moment he felt completely helpless, then instinct took over. He pulled out his phone and called Varun. "Varun!" The panic in his voice immediately alarmed him. "What happened?"

"It's Aashna."

"What?"

"She's unconscious."

"I'm taking her to the hospital."

"I'm coming."

The call ended. Without wasting another second, Rishikesh carefully lifted Aashna into his arms and carried her downstairs. She felt frighteningly light, as if life itself had already begun slipping away from her.

Outside, he stopped an auto-rickshaw and climbed inside while holding her close. The driver sped toward the hospital, for several minutes only the sound of the engine filled the silence. Then suddenly Aashna stirred, a faint movement.

Rishikesh immediately looked down. "Aashna?"

Her eyelids fluttered weakly as she slowly opened her eyes. The first thing she saw was him. A weak smile appeared on her lips, even in pain, even now.

"You are very stubborn." Her voice was barely audible "Didn't I tell you to leave?"

A tear slipped down Rishikesh's cheek. "High of you to think I would."

A faint laugh escaped her. The laugh quickly dissolved into exhaustion. Rishikesh tightened his grip around her hand and said "Nothing is going to happen to you." his voice trembled. "I'm here."

Aashna looked at him quietly. For a moment she seemed at peace, the kind of peace that frightened him.

Then she whispered softly, "Now I don't care if anything happens to me."

His heart stopped. "Don't say that."

Aashna smiled weakly. "Because you're with me."

Rishikesh looked away immediately. Unable to bear hearing those words, unable to stop the tears gathering in his eyes.

The hospital arrived, Rishikesh spotted Varun as he was already waiting near the entrance. Together they rushed Aashna inside. Doctors immediately wheeled her into the emergency ward, several nurses surrounded her, questions were asked, instructions were shouted, machines began beeping, everything happened too quickly.

Rishikesh and Varun stood outside helplessly.

A few minutes later a doctor emerged. "It's time for delivery." Her eyes scanned the hallway. "Where is her husband?" Before Rishikesh could speak, Varun stepped forward. "I called him from the reception." The doctor nodded. "He should arrive quickly." Then she disappeared back inside.

The waiting began.

The most painful waiting of Rishikesh's life.

About twenty minutes later, a man entered the hospital hurriedly.

Zaid.

Rishikesh recognized him immediately. The expensive clothes, the confident posture, the face he had imagined countless times, the man who had taken Aashna away, the man who had hurt her, the man responsible for the child she carried.bHatred surged through every vein in his body, his fists clenched automatically. If Varun hadn't been standing beside him, he might have lost control.

Zaid approached them, he looked confused and concerned. Yet strangely composed.

"You brought her here?"

Before Rishikesh could answer, Varun intervened.

"We were passing nearby and we heard her calling for help.. So we brought her here."

Zaid nodded "Thank you." His voice remained calm, professional. As though discussing a case, not his wife, not the mother of his child. Something about it disgusted Rishikesh.

"We'll stay until the baby is born," Varun added politely.

Zaid nodded again. "Thank you."

Time crawled forward, an hour passed, then another. Eventually Zaid's parents arrived, his relatives followed. Aashna's Parents would arrive by evening due to the distance.

The waiting area slowly filled. Yet through everything, Rishikesh could think only about Aashna, the woman lying beyond those doors, fighting alone, again. His stress increased with every passing minute.

Meanwhile Zaid remained seated. Quiet, expressionless, as though merely completing an obligation. The sight made Rishikesh sick.

Then finally the doors opened, a doctor emerged.

A tiny baby rested carefully in her arms. The newborn's cries echoed throughout the corridor. Everyone stood up immediately, the doctor smiled gently "Congratulations." She handed the baby to Zaid "It's a girl."

The tiny child looked impossibly small, tiny hands, tiny feet, tiny fingers curled into fragile fists. A new life, a piece of Aashna.

For a brief moment nobody spoke.

Then the doctor's expression changed. The smile disappeared and silence followed. A terrible silence.

"But..." The word froze the entire corridor. "We couldn't save your wife." Everything stopped. "She suffered severe complications during childbirth which led to postpartum hemorrhage."

"We tried our best, we're sorry."

Rishikesh stared at the doctor. Unable to understand or process or even breathe.

No. No. No.

This wasn't possible. She had been speaking to him barely hours ago, she had smiled, she had held his hand, she had kissed his forehead. What did they mean they couldn't save her?

His legs moved before his mind could catch up, he walked toward the ward, opened the door and froze. Aashna lay motionless upon the hospital bed. Peaceful, silent, gone. The machines had stopped, the struggle had ended, the woman he loved more than life itself was no longer there. Something inside him shattered irreversibly.

Before anyone could notice his reaction, Varun grabbed his shoulder and pulled him outside. They moved toward a deserted corner of the corridor.

Rishikesh finally broke. "What do you mean don't react?" His voice cracked, his entire body trembled. "I lost her." tears streamed down his face "My love, my Aashna...she's gone." The words came out between sobs.

Varun pulled him into a tight embrace. For several moments neither spoke, then Varun whispered, "I know." Rishikesh buried his face against his shoulder, completely shattered.

"I know." Varun's own eyes had filled. "But listen to me."

Rishikesh shook his head, unable to listen, unable to think.

"If people find out about you and Aashna, they'll talk." Varun continued carefully. "They'll question her, they'll insult her character, they'll call her names."

Rishikesh looked up. Broken and confused trying to comprehend what he was explaining because he was too stunned by the news.

Varun held his shoulders firmly. "Don't respect Zaid." His voice hardened "Respect Aashna."

The words struck deeply. Because even after death, she deserved dignity, she deserved peace. Slowly, painfully, Rishikesh nodded. Later, Varun offered condolences to the family. Words were exchanged, formalities completed, people cried, relatives gathered.

The world continued moving. But for Rishikesh, everything had stopped. He walked out of the hospital alone. The night air felt cold, merciless, empty, much like him.

He kept walking without direction, without purpose without even knowing where he was going. Then suddenly his legs gave way. He collapsed onto his knees beside the road, the grief he had been holding back finally exploded. A raw, broken cry escaped his chest.

"Why?" His voice echoed into the darkness. "Why?"

Tears blurred his vision. "I lost her." His hands trembled violently.

"God..." A bitter laugh escaped him. "I never believed in you." Another sob followed. "But she did." his voice cracked completely

"She believed in you."

"Then why?"

"Why did you make her suffer?"

"Why did you take away the only person who deserved happiness?"

He lowered his head his shoulders shook uncontrollably.

"Why didn't destiny let us be together?" The question vanished into the silent night but no answer came. Only the sound of a broken man crying for the woman he loved the most,

But lost her, forever.

CHAPTER TWENTY-FIVE

LOST HER.. FOREVER

Morning arrived, but it brought no relief.

The sky above Bhaderwah remained grey and heavy, as if the mountains themselves had joined in mourning. Inside the house, grief had settled into every wall, every corner, every breath people took. Relatives moved quietly, speaking in hushed voices. Some recited prayers. Some cried openly. Some simply sat in silence, unable to find words for a loss that felt too cruel to explain.

Near the center of the room lay Aashna.

Still.

Silent.

Wrapped in white.

The same girl who once laughed at the smallest things. The same girl who dreamed of becoming a writer. The same girl who wanted her words to reach the world long after she was gone.

And now she had gone before her words ever could.

Beside her sat her mother. Broken, completely broken. Her trembling fingers repeatedly brushed Aashna's forehead, as though hoping her daughter would wake up if she touched her enough times.

"Aashna..." she whispered through tears. "Get up, beta... please get up."

But the room remained silent. The daughter she had protected whenever she could. The daughter whose tears she had secretly wiped away. The daughter she had helplessly watched suffer under circumstances she could never change.

Was gone.

Every few minutes another cry echoed through the house. Not from the mourners, not from the relatives but from the newborn baby.

A tiny girl who had entered the world only to lose her mother on the very same day. The child cried without understanding what had happened, without knowing that the arms meant to hold her forever would never hold her even once, without knowing that her first day in this world had become her mother's last.

The sound shattered everyone who heard it.

Especially Rishikesh.

He stood outside the house for several minutes before gathering enough courage to step inside. Varun had tried stopping him.

"Rishi, don't do this to yourself."

But Rishikesh had only shaken his head. "I need to see her." His voice had carried no anger, no stubbornness, only pain. "I need to see her one last time."

Seeing there was no changing his mind, Varun had accompanied him. Now both stood among the crowd.

For a moment Rishikesh couldn't move. His eyes remained fixed on Aashna, his Aashna, lying there as though asleep.

For a brief second, his heart played a cruel trick on him. He imagined her opening her eyes, looking at him, smiling, scolding him. "Rishi, where were you, why did you come so late?" The image felt so real that his chest tightened. Then reality struck like a stab of knife.

She would never open her eyes again, never smile again, never tease him again, never call him "Rishi" again. He would never hear her laughter, never hear her voice, never watch her dreams unfold.

The finality of it crushed him. Slowly he walked toward her and sat beside her. Nobody stopped or questioned him because to everyone else, he was merely another mourner. But to him, she was everything.

His trembling hand reached forward before stopping midway. He wanted to touch her yet he couldn't. The reality felt unbearable. Tears slowly escaped his eyes as he looked at her face.

Beautiful as always.

There was an unusual calm upon it, the kind of peace people spend entire lives searching for. Looking at her, one would never guess how much she had suffered. How many battles she had fought, how many tears she had hidden, how many dreams had been stolen from her.

Rishikesh lowered his gaze. A broken smile appeared on his lips as he whispered softly, almost to himself,

"May no lover ever face such a day." his voice trembled. "May no heart ever have to bury the person it beats for."

The words disappeared into the silence around him. For a few moments more he simply sat there, memorizing her, trying desperately to hold onto every detail, every feature. As though forgetting even one thing would be another betrayal.

Then the preparations began. People got up and gathered there, instructions were exchanged. The time for the final rites had arrived, the crowd slowly moved forward. Someone gently asked people to step back. Rishikesh stood, his legs felt weak, heavy, almost unwilling to obey him yet he stepped away.

One step.

Then another.

Until he stood among the crowd and watched helplessly as they prepared to take her away. The distance between them increased. Just as it always had.

Aashna's body was lifted, prayers echoed around him. Some cried loudly while others wiped silent tears. The tiny cries of her daughter still lingered somewhere behind.

Rishikesh stood frozen, unable to move, unable to think, unable to accept what his eyes were witnessing. His love was being carried away from him forever.

The procession slowly moved toward the graveyard.

And he remained standing there.

A stranger among mourners or maybe the only lover among strangers. Watching from a distance as the woman he loved disappeared from his world for the final time. And in that moment, only one thought remained inside him—

"Jo meri zindagi ke har lafz me hain,
Wo kyun khamosh hai purani tasveer ki tarah..
Jiske wajood se raushan hai muqaddar mera,
Wo kyun dhal raha hai sham-e-peher ki tarah..
Mere samne uth raha hai meri mohabbat ka janaza,
Mai shareek bhi hua to gair ki tarah.."

CHAPTER TWENTY-SIX

NOTHING LEFT

The days following Aashna's funeral passed like a blur. Rishikesh no longer knew what day it was or what purpose there was in waking up. The world around him continued moving as if nothing had happened. People laughed. Shops opened. Vehicles passed. Children played in the streets.

Yet for him, time had stopped the moment Aashna closed her eyes forever. Every morning he found himself wandering toward Seoj Meadow, the same place where he had seen her again after more than a year, the same place where destiny had returned her to him. Only to snatch her away once more.

That afternoon he sat alone beneath a coniferous tree overlooking the valley. The mountains stretched endlessly before him, but he wasn't looking at them. His eyes were fixed somewhere far beyond, lost among memories.

He remembered the way she had looked at him in the hospital auto. "Now I don't care if anything happens to me, because you're with me."

The memory stabbed him.

A tear slipped down his face, he wiped it away mechanically. There seemed little point in crying anymore because his heart had already broken beyond repair.

The sound of approaching footsteps pulled him from his thoughts. At first he ignored them then a familiar voice spoke.

"Beta... are you Rishikesh?" He looked up.

Standing before him was Aashna's mother. For a moment he was too surprised to speak.

Slowly he stood. "Ji."

She stared at him for a few moments before tears filled her eyes.

"I knew it." Her voice trembled. "I noticed you on the funeral day."

Rishikesh remained silent.

She continued softly, "Something in my heart kept telling me that you were him."

"Him?" he asked quietly.

"The boy my daughter loved."

The words shattered whatever strength he still possessed. Aashna's mother lowered her gaze.

"My daughter loved you very much, son." Her eyes filled with tears "Very, very much."

Rishikesh looked away immediately, unable to bear hearing those words now. Not after losing her.

Aashna's mother sat beside him, for several moments neither spoke.

Then she whispered, "On the day of her mehendi, the artist wrote her fiancé's name on her hand." Her voice cracked. "When she saw it, she locked herself inside a room." Rishikesh listened silently.

"She scrubbed her skin until it started bleeding." A sob escaped her "Just to remove his name."

Rishikesh lowered his head, his shoulders trembled. Every new thing he learned about Aashna's suffering felt like another knife twisting inside him.

"She kept saying she belonged only to you."

The sentence broke him completely. Tears streamed freely down his face. For a long time neither spoke, only the wind moved through the trees. Eventually Aashna's mother wiped her eyes.

"I wanted to help her." Her voice was filled with regret. "I wanted her to marry you."

Rishikesh looked toward her.

"But her father..." The woman immediately shook her head.

"No." Rishikesh's voice hardened. "Please don't call him her father." His jaw clenched "He doesn't deserve that word."

For the first time, she didn't argue. Instead, she looked down.

"I couldn't do anything, beta." Her voice carried years of helplessness. "I was a widow with a little girl." She stared toward the mountains. "When he married me, I thought our lives would become better." A painful smile appeared on her lips. "He gave us a home, gave us a name."

"I thought Aashna would finally have stability."

The smile vanished. "But he never accepted her."

The confession carried decades of pain. Rishikesh felt anger rising again, toward the man, toward fate, toward everything.

Then Aashna's mother slowly joined her hands before him.

The gesture startled him. "Aunty..." But she didn't lower them.

"Please." Her voice broke. "I need to ask something from you."

Rishikesh looked at her silently.

She took a shaky breath. "Take Aashna's daughter with you."

The world seemed to pause.

"What?"

"Please."

Fresh tears rolled down her cheeks. "Otherwise she'll suffer the same fate as Aashna."

Rishikesh froze. The request felt impossible.

"You're a good man." Aashna's mother continued desperately. "I know you are and I trust you more than I trust Zaid, who will take care of her when I'll go back to Aragam" she continued "What if they put her to adoption"

"You'll love her, you'll raise her as your own." Her folded hands trembled. "Please don't let that child grow up where my daughter suffered."

Rishikesh stared at the ground, the words reached him. But they couldn't stay. His mind was already drowning beneath too much pain. Finally he shook his head, slowly and weakly.

"I'm sorry." His voice sounded hollow. "I can't."

The woman's eyes widened.

Rishikesh swallowed hard. "I have no will to live."

The confession surprised even him yet it was true.

"I have no purpose, no direction, no answers." He looked toward the valley. "I can't even take care of myself right now." His voice cracked. "How can I take responsibility for a child?"

The silence that followed felt unbearable.

Aashna's mother lowered her hands. She didn't argue because she could see the devastation written across his face. This wasn't selfishness, this was a man who had lost everything.

"I'm sorry," he repeated quietly.

Then he turned away, leaving behind a grieving mother, and a newborn child.

That evening he returned to Varun's house, his bag was already packed before dinner.

Varun noticed immediately. "Where are you going?"

Rishikesh zipped the bag shut "I don't know."

"What?" A faint, lifeless smile appeared on his face.

"I genuinely don't know."

Varun stared at him.

"Rishi..."

"Wherever life takes me."

The answer frightened Varun because it sounded less like a journey and more like surrender. The following morning he left Bhaderwah. No destination, no plan, no future, only memories.

Days turned into weeks, weeks turned into months. Sometimes he travelled by bus, sometimes by train and sometimes simply on foot. He wandered from town to town like a man searching for something he could never find.

Some days he spent without eating a single grain of food. Other nights he slept wherever he found space, railway stations, bus stands, temple courtyards, park benches, anywhere.

Every road eventually led back to the same place, Aashna. Every sunset reminded him of her, every bookstore reminded him of her, every letter he saw reminded him of her. Sometimes he imagined hearing her voice, sometimes he turned around expecting to see her standing behind him, sometimes he even forgot she was gone.

Only for reality to strike again moments later. The pain never lessened, it simply became part of him. People around him continued living, dreaming, loving, planning futures.

Meanwhile Rishikesh existed like a shadow. Breathing, walking, surviving but not living. Because somewhere deep inside, a part of him had been buried beside Aashna. And it had never returned.

CHAPTER TWENTY-SEVEN

The Reason to Live

Months of wandering eventually brought Rishikesh back to the city that carried his own name.

Rishikesh.

The irony wasn't lost on him.

Once, he had imagined returning here with Aashna. He had imagined showing her the ghats, sitting beside the river with her, listening to her endless stories while the evening aarti echoed across the water.

Now he had returned alone.

The city felt unfamiliar despite being home. The streets seemed quieter, the colors seemed duller or perhaps the world itself had not changed, perhaps it was him.

That evening he found himself walking aimlessly along the banks of the Ganga. Pilgrims moved around him. Priests chanted prayers. Children ran after one another. Somewhere bells rang from a nearby temple.

Life continued, as if nothing had happened, as if a girl named Aashna had never existed. As if she had not carried a universe inside her. As if she had not been his entire world.

Rishikesh stepped onto the stone stairs leading into the river. The water was cold. He took another step, then another. The river rose to his knees, then his waist and then his chest.

People around him continued with their prayers, paying little attention.

The current gently brushed against him, inviting him deeper. For the first time in months, his mind felt strangely quiet, no questions, no regrets, no expectations , only exhaustion.

He closed his eyes and Aashna appeared immediately, just as she always did. Standing beneath the rain in her purple kurti, smiling, teasing him, running her fingers through his hair while he rested his head in her lap, kissing his forehead, calling him "Rishi", then laying lifeless with closed eyes.

His chest tightened, he took another step. The water rose above his shoulders, then his neck.

Then finally— Everything disappeared beneath the river.

Silence.

Rishikesh remained underwater with his eyes closed, body still. The river wrapped around him like a blanket. Perhaps this was easier, perhaps this was what surrender felt like. He thought about Aashna, about the life they never got to live, about the home they never built, about the daughter who would grow up without knowing her mother, about every dream that had died with her.

His lungs slowly began demanding air, an uncomfortable pressure formed inside his chest. Instinct begged him to rise, to breathe, to survive.

But he refused.

The pressure intensified, his chest burned, his body struggled against his decision.

Still he refused. A few more seconds, just a few more.

Then suddenly— A child cried. The sound reached him even through the water, faint yet unmistakable. A baby's cry. Rishikesh's eyes opened instantly, for a moment he thought he had imagined it but then the cry came again, louder and desperate.

Something inside him reacted before he could stop it. His body surged upward, he emerged from the river gasping for air. The world returned all at once, noise' voices, breath, life. He stood there breathing heavily while searching for the source of the sound.

A few steps away, a young woman was trying desperately to comfort a crying infant. The baby continued sobbing, tiny hands reaching outward, tiny face red from crying, the sight struck him like lightning.

Aashna's daughter. The image appeared immediately in his mind, the child he had left behind, the child whose mother had died, the child Aashna had loved before even seeing her face.

For the first time since Aashna's death, something stronger than grief entered his heart.

Guilt.

What was that little girl doing right now? Who was holding her? Who was comforting her? Would anyone love her the way Aashna would have?

The questions refused to leave.

And suddenly drowning no longer seemed important because there was someone else who had lost Aashna too, someone even more helpless than him.

Rishikesh slowly walked out of the river, water dripped from his clothes. His hands trembled but his decision was already made.

He needed to go back.

Immediately.

The journey to Bhaderwah felt longer than before. For the first time in months, he was moving toward something rather than away from it.

The next evening he stood outside Aashna's house once again. The same house where he had last seen her alive, the same house from where she had left for her wedding, the same house that now felt unbearably empty. He remained standing near the back entrance quietly.

Moments later, someone noticed him. Aashna's mother. The moment she saw him, surprise appeared across her face, then hope. She hurried toward him.

"Rishikesh?"

He nodded.

For a few moments neither spoke.

Then he finally managed, "I've changed my decision."

The woman stared at him.

His eyes filled with tears. "I want to take her with me."

For a moment she simply stood there. Then tears rolled down her cheeks, not from grief but from relief. She looked toward the sky briefly as if silently thanking God.

"I knew you'd come back."

Rishikesh lowered his gaze. "I almost didn't."

The woman understood without asking. She had seen the brokenness in his eyes, she knew where he had been, mentally and emotionally.

After a few moments she whispered, "Come after midnight."

Rishikesh nodded.

The house fell silent as the night deepened, one by one the lights went out. The relatives slept, the town slept. Only two people remained awake. A grieving grandmother and a grieving lover.

When the clock crossed midnight, Rishikesh quietly returned. Aashna's mother opened the door without a word. Everything had already been prepared. A small bag containing baby clothes, a blanket, milk bottles, tiny necessities and a diary that belonged to Aashna.

The entire life of a child packed into a single bundle. Then she carefully lifted the sleeping baby into his arms. For the first time, Rishikesh held her, she felt impossibly small, impossibly fragile. As if the slightest mistake could break her, he looked down at her sleeping face and his heart tightened. Aashna had held this child for only a few moments then destiny had separated them forever.

Rishikesh adjusted his hold protectively as though carrying something sacred, something precious, something entrusted to him by fate itself. Aashna's mother gently kissed the baby's forehead. Tears streamed down her cheeks.

"Take care of her."

Rishikesh nodded, unable to speak. Then he turned and walked away carrying the little girl. Hours later they were sitting inside a bus, most passengers slept. The road stretched endlessly through the darkness. For a long time the baby remained asleep, Rishikesh simply watched her, afraid to even blink.

Then slowly she stirred, tiny fingers moved and her eyes opened. And the moment he saw them, his breath caught. They were Aashna's eyes, the same depth, the same softness, the same innocence. For several seconds he simply stared, unable to believe it.

The baby looked at him curiously then suddenly she giggled. A tiny, innocent laugh, the smallest sound imaginable yet it shattered months of darkness. A smile appeared on Rishikesh's face, his first genuine smile since Aashna's death.

The little girl reached toward him with her tiny hand and as Rishikesh gently held it, he realized something. For months he had been searching for a reason to stay alive perhaps destiny had been carrying that reason in its arms all along.

CHAPTER TWENTY-EIGHT

A Life Worth Living

The journey back to Rishikesh felt different from every journey Rishikesh had taken during the past year.

For the first time, he wasn't travelling alone.

The tiny child sleeping peacefully in his arms occasionally moved in her sleep, curling her fingers around his shirt as if afraid he might disappear. Every time she did that, he found himself looking at her for a few seconds longer than necessary.

The resemblance was impossible to ignore. Sometimes it was her eyes, sometimes the shape of her smile, sometimes simply the way she slept. Each reminder hurt yet somehow, each reminder healed too.

By the time the bus entered the city, dawn had begun spreading across the sky. The roads were slowly coming alive. Tea vendors were opening their stalls and morning prayers echoed from distant temples.

Rishikesh tightened his hold around the baby.

He was finally going home.

When he reached his house and knocked on the door, his mother opened it almost immediately. The moment she saw him, relief crossed her face.

Then confusion.

Then shock.

"Rishi?" Her eyes immediately moved toward the baby sleeping in his arms. "What is this?"

Before she could ask another question, she noticed his appearance properly. His unshaven face, the dark circles beneath his eyes, the exhaustion, the sadness. Something had happened, something terrible. A mother's heart understood before words did.

She quickly moved aside and let him enter. Inside, his elder brother and sister-in-law also woke up after hearing the commotion. Everyone gathered in the living room, staring at the child and then at Rishikesh.

Questions flooded from every direction.

"Whose baby is this?"

"Where were you all these months?"

"What happened?"

"Why do you look like this?"

Rishikesh remained silent. For a long time. Then he sat down slowly, the child still asleep in his arms. And for the first time since Aashna's death, he began telling someone everything.

"Maa..." His voice cracked immediately. He looked down, gathering courage and then continued. "I fell in love with a girl."

The room became silent.

He told them about the library, the letters, the rain, the confession, the separation, the missed letters, the forced marriage, the reunion, the pregnancy, the hospital, the funeral.

Everything.

Every wound he had been carrying alone, every memory, every regret, every tear. As he spoke, his mother covered her mouth to stop herself from crying. His sister-in-law wiped her eyes repeatedly. Even his brother remained silent.

Nobody interrupted, nobody judged, they simply listened.

And when he finally reached the part where Aashna died, his voice broke completely. The strength he had somehow maintained for months disappeared. The walls around his heart collapsed. For the first time since returning, he cried. Not quietly or silently. He broke down completely like a child.

His mother immediately sat beside him and pulled him into her arms. The way mothers do, the way only mothers can. And suddenly he wasn't the strong man carrying everyone's burden, he was simply a son who had come home after surviving a storm.

Rishikesh buried his face against her shoulder and cried until there were no tears left. His mother stroked his hair gently. The same way she had done when he was little.

"My child..." Her voice trembled. "How much pain were you carrying all alone?"

The question only made him cry harder. After several minutes she looked toward the sleeping baby. Then carefully lifted her into her own lap. The child stirred slightly before settling comfortably.

His mother smiled through tears. "No child deserves to grow up without love."

She kissed the baby's forehead. Then looked at Rishikesh. "If this is your decision, then she is our daughter too."

Fresh tears appeared in his eyes.

His mother smiled. "We will raise her together."

Then she kissed the baby again. "My little doll, meri gudiya."

For the first time in a very long while, Rishikesh felt something he thought he had lost forever.

Home.

The following morning, everyone gathered around the dining table discussing names. Suggestions came from every direction but Rishikesh already knew. There had only ever been one name.

"Kehkasha."

Everyone looked toward him. A small smile appeared on his lips.

"It was Aashna's favourite name." His fingers gently touched the baby's tiny hand. "She once told me if she ever published poetry, she wanted to do it under this name."

His mother nodded immediately. "Then Kehkasha it is."

And just like that, Aashna's dream found a way to remain alive. The months that followed transformed Rishikesh completely. The man who once wanted to drown himself in the Ganga now woke up multiple times every night because Kehkasha refused to sleep.

He learned how to prepare milk, how to change diapers, how to carry her without waking her, how to calm her when she cried, how to recognize the difference between hunger and discomfort. Some mornings he arrived late to work because she refused to stop crying, some nights he stayed awake until sunrise because she had a fever.

Yet he never complained, not even once. Because every difficult moment reminded him that she was here.

Alive, safe and loved.

He worked during the day, returned home as quickly as possible, played with her, fed her, made her laugh, put her to sleep and repeated the same routine again the next day.

Slowly his entire world began revolving around her

Years passed quietly.

Kehkasha took her first steps while holding his finger.

Lost her first tooth.

Fell while learning to ride a bicycle.

Every milestone felt more precious than the last. And every time she achieved something, Rishikesh wished Aashna could see it. Sometimes he even caught himself speaking to her photograph. "Did you see that, Aashi? Our daughter is growing so fast."

Then one evening, when Kehkasha was barely old enough to speak properly, she came running toward him with unsteady little steps. Rishikesh crouched down with open arms. The little girl smiled brightly.

Then spoke "Papa."

The single word froze him. For a moment he couldn't move, couldn't breathe, couldn't think. Then tears filled his eyes. He lifted her immediately into his arms and held her tightly. The little girl giggled, not understanding why her father was crying.

But Rishikesh knew.

Because in that moment, she had given him something he never expected to have.

A family.

The years continued passing.

Kehkasha grew into a bright and intelligent young girl. Every morning Rishikesh dropped her at school. Every afternoon she came running out of the gate searching for him. The moment she spotted him, she would run straight into his arms and no matter how busy he was, he was always there.

Always, unlike fate, unlike destiny, unlike life itself.

Rishikesh never left.

CHAPTER TWENTY-NINE

Words That Finally Reached

Life slowly settled into a rhythm around Kehkasha. The years that had once felt impossible to survive now passed quietly between school uniforms, bedtime stories, scraped knees, parent-teacher meetings, and countless small moments that stitched themselves into Rishikesh's heart. Yet amidst all the responsibilities of fatherhood, there remained one promise he had made to himself—a promise he had never spoken aloud to anyone.

Aashna deserved to be read.

Whenever Kehkasha slept, he would sit beside the small study table in his room and open the worn-out notebook that contained Aashna's poems. Some pages had faded ink. Some carried tear stains. Some had little doodles she had absent-mindedly drawn in the corners. Every page felt alive with her presence.

One night, after staring at those poems for hours, he finally made a decision.

He would publish them.

The next few months were spent compiling her work, arranging poems, writing descriptions, and preparing a manuscript. When it was finally complete, he sent it to a publisher with trembling hands.

The rejection arrived two weeks later.

"Unfortunately, this manuscript does not align with our current publishing requirements."

Rishikesh read the email twice before quietly closing the screen.

Then he sent it elsewhere.

Another rejection.

Then another.

Then another.

Then another.

Five publishers.

Five rejections.

Anyone else might have given up but he knew Aashna. She would never have stopped trying, so neither would he.

During those days he began writing his own stories as well. He would return from work, spend time with Kehkasha, put her to sleep, and then write until late in the night. Sometimes exhaustion made his eyes burn. Sometimes he fell asleep at the table itself. Yet every morning he woke up and continued.

His first novel was finally accepted by a small publishing house.

The day he held the printed copy in his hands, he smiled. Not because it was perfect but because it existed.

Months passed.

Sales were disappointing.

The reviews were average.

The book disappeared almost as quietly as it had arrived.

His second book performed slightly better.

His third barely sold.

Still he continued writing.

Every story he wrote carried pieces of grief he could never speak aloud.

Then one night, while sorting old papers, he came across a sunflower pressed between two notebook pages. A memory struck him instantly, the girl who wanted people to notice her work and not her.

He sat down and began writing. Not fiction, not imagination, not inspiration.

The truth.

For the first time, he wrote about Aashna. About the letters, about rain-soaked mornings, about waiting, about losing, about loving someone beyond death itself.

The manuscript took almost a year to complete. When he finally sent it to a publisher, he expected another rejection. Instead, they called him, then another publisher called, then another.

For the first time in his life, people wanted to read his words.

The novel was published.

And within months, it exploded in popularity. Readers connected with the emotions, young lovers cried reading it, parents wrote letters to him, students quoted passages from it online, bookstores sold out copies repeatedly.

Interviews followed, literary festivals followed, recognition followed.

Suddenly, Rishikesh was no longer just a struggling writer. He had become one of the most talked-about authors in the country. Yet whenever anyone congratulated him, his thoughts always returned to one person, aashna.

The girl who had taught him the power of words, the girl whose story the world was finally reading.

A few years later, using the influence he had gained, he fulfilled the promise he had carried for so long. Aashna's poetry collection was finally published.

The first copy arrived at his home on a quiet evening. He stared at the cover for several moments then gently placed it before her photograph.

"Aashi you told me na I too should have a dream..," he whispered.

His eyes glistened.

"I have a dream of fulfilling your dreams, You become a published writer Aashna."

For a moment he could almost imagine her smiling back.

Time continued moving forward.

Before he realised it, the tiny child he had once carried through a midnight bus journey had become a young woman.

The day of Kehkasha's high school graduation arrived.

The auditorium buzzed with excitement. Proud parents filled the seats while students adjusted their gowns and took photographs with friends. Rishikesh sat quietly among hundreds of families, camera in hand, unable to believe how quickly the years had passed.

Then the principal announced the student speaker.

"Kehkasha Rishikesh Mehra."

The hall erupted in applause. Rishikesh smiled proudly as his daughter walked toward the podium. She looked confident, graceful and strong.

For a brief second she reminded him so much of Aashna that his chest tightened.

Kehkasha unfolded her speech and looked toward the audience.

"I was asked to speak about motherhood today."

The hall fell silent.

Rishikesh listened attentively.

"I never knew my biological mother. I was too young to remember her. For many years, I felt sad about it. I wondered what it would feel like to have a mother waiting for me after school, helping me with homework, or comforting me when life became difficult."

Her voice trembled slightly.

Then she smiled.

"But as I grew older, I realised something. Motherhood is not just about giving birth. Motherhood is about protection. Sacrifice. Comfort. Unconditional love."

Rishikesh felt his throat tighten.

Kehkasha looked directly toward him.

"And I received all of those things from my father."

The audience turned toward him.

Rishikesh lowered his gaze, already emotional.

"My father never allowed me to feel incomplete. He attended every school event. He learned to braid my hair. He sacrificed dreams, sleep, comfort, and sometimes even his own happiness to make sure I never lacked love."

His vision blurred.

The hall disappeared behind tears.

"When I was scared, he protected me. When I failed, he encouraged me. When I succeeded, he celebrated louder than anyone else. People often ask me what kind of man I want to marry someday."

A small laugh echoed through the auditorium.

Kehkasha smiled.

"My answer is simple. Someone half as good as my father."

The audience burst into applause.

Rishikesh wiped his eyes completely defeated by emotion.

By the time the ceremony ended, he was still trying to compose himself.

The moment Kehkasha spotted him outside, she ran toward him exactly the way she had when she was a little girl returning from school.

Without caring about the crowd around them, she threw her arms around him.

"Papa!"

Rishikesh hugged her, prouder than he had ever been.

She pulled back slightly and looked into his eyes.

"I couldn't have asked for a better father."

Fresh tears appeared instantly.

Kehkasha smiled.

"You are the best man in the world."

For a moment Rishikesh couldn't speak. He simply held her again.

And somewhere deep within his heart, he felt that if Aashna could see this moment, she would be proud too.

The girl who once feared she would never leave behind a legacy had left behind something far greater than books.

She had left behind love.

CHAPTER THIRTY

Traces of the Past

Success had arrived in Rishikesh's life quietly. It wasn't a single moment, not a single award, not a single bestseller. It was years of words finally reaching where they were meant to.

His novel Aakhri Khat: Part One had become a literary phenomenon. Readers discussed it online, universities prescribed passages from it for discussion, and thousands of letters arrived every month from people who saw pieces of their own lives in his writing.

Ironically, the man whose love story had once been destroyed by letters now spent his days receiving them.

One winter morning, Rishikesh received an invitation from a prestigious university. They wanted him as the chief guest for their annual literary festival. Normally he avoided public appearances but something about the invitation reminded him of his younger days.

So he accepted.

The university auditorium was packed.

Students filled every seat. Some stood near walls simply to catch a glimpse of him. Large posters of his books decorated the entrance while volunteers rushed around trying to manage the crowd.

When Rishikesh finally walked onto the stage, the hall erupted into applause. He smiled politely and adjusted the microphone.

For a moment he looked at the sea of young faces before him. Faces filled with ambition, hope and possibilities. Faces that reminded him of a younger version of himself.

Then he began speaking. "I often get asked how to become a writer."

The auditorium fell silent.

"The truth is, writing isn't about becoming famous, It's about surviving yourself."

The hall remained attentive.

"I wrote because I had things I couldn't say aloud. I wrote because sometimes paper understands pain better than people do. Every rejection taught me patience. Every failure taught me resilience. If you wish to write, then don't chase success. Chase honesty."

The students listened carefully.

"Because readers don't remember perfect sentences. They remember genuine emotions."

A loud applause followed.

For almost an hour he spoke about literature, storytelling, rejection, discipline, and the responsibility of writing truthfully.

By the time he stepped off the stage, dozens of students surrounded him for photographs and autographs. Despite his age, he greeted everyone patiently, signed books, answered questions and encouraged aspiring writers.

Eventually the crowd began thinning. That was when a young man approached him, he couldn't have been older than twenty. A notebook rested beneath his arm while excitement shone clearly on his face.

"Sir."

Rishikesh turned.

The young man smiled nervously.

"I'm Hriday."

"Hello, Hriday."

The boy looked as though he couldn't believe he was standing in front of his favorite author.

"Sir, your books changed my life."

Rishikesh chuckled softly. "That's a dangerous thing to tell a writer."

The boy laughed. "I mean it."

There was something sincere about him. Something genuine. The kind of sincerity that couldn't be faked. For several minutes they spoke about books and writing. To Rishikesh's surprise, Hriday was remarkably insightful, he understood literature deeply, he asked thoughtful questions, he listened carefully. Most importantly, he possessed the hunger every good writer carried. The hunger to understand people.

Eventually one of the event organizers approached.

"Sir, your car is ready."

Rishikesh checked his watch. He had another commitment in the city.

"I'm sorry, Hriday. I'd stay longer, but I have to leave."

The disappointment on the boy's face was immediate. "Oh."

Rishikesh smiled. "Come visit me after two days."

Hriday blinked. "What?"

"My house."

The boy looked stunned.

Rishikesh scribbled an address on a piece of paper.

"We'll talk properly there."

Hriday seemed speechless. "Thank you, sir."

Rishikesh simply smiled and left.

Two days later, Hriday stood outside Rishikesh's house. The same house where countless novels had been written.

Rishikesh welcomed him warmly.

Books occupied nearly every wall of the house. Manuscripts lay stacked on shelves, photographs from literary events decorated one corner.

Hriday looked around like a child entering a wonderland. "This is incredible."

Rishikesh laughed. "It's mostly clutter."

For the next few hours they talked endlessly about writing, literature, publishing, failure, success. Hriday listened carefully to every word.

Then the conversation shifted toward the past.

"Sir," Hriday asked, "what were you like in college?"

Rishikesh smiled. "A menace."

Hriday laughed. "You?"

"I was constantly getting into trouble."

The answer surprised him. They continued talking.

Then Hriday picked up a copy of Aakhri Khat from the table and asked

"When the part two of Akhiri Khat is coming?"

"Shortly, only the last letter is left"

"Sir, Can I ask one more thing?"

"Hm?"

"The characters in this book."

Rishikesh immediately knew where this was going.

"They're fictional."

Hriday nodded. "But they're not."

The room became quiet. Rishikesh leaned back slightly.

"They are."

"No."

The certainty in Hriday's voice was unsettling. "I know they're real."

Rishikesh's smile disappeared. Years of practice had taught him how to avoid this discussion. The public loved speculating but he never confirmed anything.

"You're reading too much into it."

"I'm not."

Something about Hriday's tone irritated him. Perhaps because it sounded too confident, too sure.

"You are diving too deep, son."

For the first time, sharpness entered his voice. The room fell silent.

Hriday looked at him carefully then lowered his gaze. For a moment Rishikesh thought the conversation was over.

Then the young man spoke.

Quietly.

Almost gently.

"I know because I know one of them."

The words made Rishikesh stiffen. His heartbeat slowed.

"What?"

Hriday looked directly into his eyes. The next sentence struck harder than any accusation ever could.

"My mother is Mrunal."

Silence, complete silence. The room vanished, the books vanished. Everything disappeared, only one name remained.

Mrunal.

Twenty-two years.

Twenty-two years had passed, yet the wound opened as though it had happened yesterday. Suddenly he was no longer sitting in his study. He was standing inside a birthday party holding unopened letters, reading Aashna's desperate pleas feeling his heart shatter.

Mrunal.

The name echoed through every memory.

His hands tightened unconsciously around the armrest. For several moments neither spoke. Hriday watched him carefully. And for the first time since arriving, he understood that the story he had admired in books wasn't merely fiction, It was grief, real grief.

Still alive after all these years.

And sitting directly in front of him.

Waiting to be remembered.

CHAPTER THIRTY-ONE

The Forgotten Chapter

The silence that followed Hriday's revelation felt suffocating.

Rishikesh remained seated in his chair, staring somewhere beyond the room, beyond the shelves lined with books and the afternoon sunlight spilling through the windows. Twenty years disappeared in an instant. The wrinkles on his face, the grey in his hair, the years he had spent building a life around Kehkasha—all of it faded behind memories he had spent decades trying to bury.

Mrunal.

The name alone was enough to reopen wounds he had convinced himself had healed. Hriday sat quietly across from him, suddenly unsure whether he should have said it.

For several moments neither spoke. The ticking of the wall clock became the loudest sound in the room. Finally, Rishikesh leaned back in his chair and closed his eyes.

"So she finally told someone."

His voice carried neither anger nor surprise, only fatigue.

Hriday lowered his gaze, "She never stopped carrying it, sir."

Rishikesh let out a hollow laugh. "Carrying it?"

The words escaped his lips before he could stop them. His eyes slowly opened.

"Do you know what she carried, Hriday?"

The young man remained silent.

Rishikesh nodded. "I'll tell you."

His voice had become calmer now, dangerously calm.

"The woman I loved waited for me till her wedding day." He paused. "She packed her luggage, she believed I would come." His fingers tightened around the armrest. "And I never knew."

The room fell silent once again. Hriday listened without interrupting.

"Do you know what haunts me the most?" Rishikesh asked.

"It isn't that Aashna died." His voice cracked slightly. "It isn't even that she got married."

A long breath escaped him. "It is knowing that she needed me and I wasn't there."

The words seemed to hurt even after all these years.

"Every night for years I wondered if she thought I abandoned her." His eyes glistened. "If she cried because of me." "If she hated me, If she spent her last days believing I never loved her enough."

Hriday swallowed hard. For the first time he was hearing the pain hidden behind the pages of Aakhri Khat. The pain readers admired, the pain that had never truly ended.

"My mother knows she made a mistake."

Rishikesh looked away. "Mistake." He repeated the word softly as though testing it.

"No, son." His gaze returned to Hriday.

"A mistake is forgetting someone's birthday."

"A mistake is sending a message to the wrong person."

His voice lowered.

"What happened wasn't a mistake."

The words hung heavily between them.

"It was a choice."

Hriday's shoulders slumped. Because deep down, he knew Rishikesh was right.

"My mother says that every day."

Rishikesh looked at him.

"Then she's more honest than most people."

The boy nodded. A painful silence followed. Then Hriday spoke again.

"She never wanted me to hate her."

Rishikesh remained expressionless.

"When I was younger, I once asked why she cried whenever she saw. your books."

The old writer looked up.

"She never answered." Hriday smiled sadly. "But I eventually found out."

His fingers brushed against the copy of Aakhri Khat lying on the table.

"She keeps every article written about you."

Rishikesh frowned.

"She says your success makes her happy." Hriday continued "And guilty."

The room once again fell silent. Outside, a gentle breeze moved through the garden. Life continued. Yet both men sat surrounded by ghosts. After a while, Hriday carefully spoke again.

"She wants to meet you."

The response came immediately. "No."

Hriday had expected it. Still, hearing it hurt.

"Sir—"

"No."

The firmness in Rishikesh's voice left little room for argument. He stood from his chair and walked toward the window. The garden stretched before him, the same garden where he often sat with a notebook when memories became unbearable. Without turning around, he spoke.

"Some chapters are better left unread."

His voice was quiet, but unwavering.

"I don't want to meet her." The words settled heavily in the room "Neither will I be able to forgive her."

Hriday looked down. He had expected resistance, just not this much pain. For several moments he considered remaining silent.

Then he stood up. Slowly, respectfully. "I understand."

Rishikesh remained facing the window.

"I truly do." His voice carried sincerity. "I understand your anger, your refusal, your pain."

The older man said nothing. Hriday took a few hesitant steps forward then stopped.

"I'm not asking you to forgive her."

Those words finally made Rishikesh turn. The young man met his eyes. There was no manipulation there, no pressure, only sincerity.

"I'm not even asking you to forget." His voice trembled slightly. "Because some things shouldn't be forgotten."

Rishikesh stared at him. For the first time, he saw not Mrunal's son but simply a young man trying to fulfill a mother's final wish.

"Then what are you asking?" he said quietly.

Hriday swallowed. A sadness appeared in his eyes. The kind of sadness that comes from watching someone suffer for years.

"Just meet her once."

The room became still.

"Please." His voice cracked. "One last time."

Rishikesh felt something shift uneasily inside him. Not forgiveness, not yet perhaps only curiosity or perhaps the exhaustion of carrying old wounds for too long.

But for the first time since hearing Mrunal's name, he found himself unable to immediately say no.

And that frightened him more than the memories themselves.

CHAPTER THIRTY-TWO

The Weight of Forgiveness

The afternoon sunlight filtered through the living room windows, painting long shadows across the floor. Rishikesh sat quietly on the sofa, a half-finished cup of tea resting on the table before him. Though he appeared calm on the outside, a storm raged within him.

A knock echoed through the house.

His fingers instinctively tightened around the armrest. He knew who it was. For a brief moment, he considered walking away but before he could, Kehkasha opened the door.

Hriday entered first and behind him walked Mrunal.

The sight of her instantly dragged him twenty years into the past. The birthday party, the letters, the grief he had carried for decades. All of it returned at once.

Mrunal looked older now. Time had touched her face just as it had touched his. There were lines around her eyes and strands of silver hidden among her hair. Yet the guilt she carried was far more visible than age itself.

For a few seconds neither spoke.

Then she offered a weak smile.

"How are you, Rishikesh?"

He looked away before answering. "Fine."

A single word, polite, distant. Nothing more.

The silence that followed felt uncomfortable. Hriday quietly settled beside his mother while Kehkasha excused herself.

Mrunal glanced around the room. Her eyes landed on the framed cover of Aakhri Khat hanging on the wall. "The book became a huge success."

Rishikesh nodded. "It did."

"I read Part One."

"Hm."

Another short reply. No warmth, no curiosity, no invitation to continue.

Mrunal lowered her gaze. She had imagined this moment countless times over the years. None of those versions had been this difficult. For several seconds she simply stared at her hands. Then finally she spoke.

"I was selfish, Rishi."

The words immediately changed the atmosphere of the room.

Rishikesh remained silent.

"I know what I did." Her voice trembled. "I know there is no justification."

Still he said nothing.

Tears slowly gathered in her eyes. "When I was younger, I convinced myself it was love." She laughed bitterly. "But it wasn't."

The confession seemed to cost her something.

"I disguised my infatuation as love." Her eyes finally lifted toward him. "I thought if Aashna disappeared from your life, maybe one day you would look at me the way you looked at her."

The room remained silent except for her voice.

"But I was wrong." A tear rolled down her cheek.

"Love is not about possessing someone, It is not about getting them. Love is about protecting their happiness, even if it does not include you."

Her voice broke completely. For the first time, Rishikesh slowly looked toward her.

Mrunal wiped her tears. "What you had for Aashna..." She smiled sadly "That was love."

The words lingered between them. "And what I did destroyed it."

Hriday sat quietly beside her listening to truths he had never heard spoken aloud.

Mrunal continued speaking through tears. "I know saying sorry does not change anything." Her hands trembled. "I know it doesn't bring back those years, erase her pain or erase yours." She struggled to continue "But I am sorry." The words came out broken. "Genuinely sorry."

Years of guilt seemed to pour out with them. "I have lived with this every day." She pressed her palms together. Not dramatically but simply because she no longer knew what else to do.

"Every time I saw your success, I felt proud." A tear escaped her eye. "And guilty." Another followed.

Her voice cracked. "I remembered what I took away."

The room had become painfully quiet. Even the ticking clock seemed louder. Mrunal lowered her head then finally asked the question she had carried for twenty years.

"Can you ever forgive me?"

The words hung heavily in the air. For a long time, Rishikesh said nothing. He looked toward the photograph resting on the shelf across the room.

Aashna.

Smiling softly from within the frame as though untouched by the tragedies that had followed. His eyes remained fixed there.

Then he spoke quietly. "If Aashna were here..." his voice softened. "She would've forgiven you long ago."

Fresh tears filled Mrunal's eyes, a faint smile appeared on his lips, painful and nostalgic.

"She was always kinder than me."

The room fell silent again. Mrunal could barely breathe. Rishikesh looked down at his hands, at the scars life had left behind, at the years that had passed, at everything he had carried for far too long.

Then he slowly raised his head. "So I'll try."

Mrunal froze.

Hriday looked up instantly.

For the first time since arriving, hope appeared in his eyes. Rishikesh exhaled deeply.

"Forgiving you won't erase my wound." His voice remained calm "It won't change what happened, It won't bring back the years we lost."

Mrunal nodded through tears.

He continued. "But carrying hatred for the rest of my life won't change those things either."

The room became still. A gentle smile finally appeared on his face, small but genuine.

"It simply means the wound no longer controls my life."

Mrunal broke down completely. Not because she deserved forgiveness but because after twenty years, the burden she had carried alone had finally become a little lighter. Beside her, Hriday smiled through moist eyes. The relief on his face was impossible to miss.

Rishikesh noticed it and smiled faintly as well.

For the first time that afternoon, the room felt lighter.

Not healed. Some wounds never fully heal, but get lighter. And somewhere in that moment, it felt as though Aashna herself would have approved.

Because love had always been the thing that connected them.

And perhaps, after all these years, it had finally become the thing that set them free.

CHAPTER THIRTY-THREE

Aakhiri Khat..

The golden rays of the setting sun filtered through the study window, casting long shadows across the room. Dust particles floated lazily in the air while stacks of manuscripts occupied every corner of the table. Beside them rested a framed photograph of Aashna, the same photograph that had accompanied Rishikesh through decades of writing, grief, and love.

Some things had remained unchanged. The way he still looked at Aashna's photograph, the way her memory still occupied the quiet corners of his heart and the way every book somehow found its way back to her.

Across the room sat the completed manuscript of Aakhri Khat: Part Two. Hundreds of pages, thousands of words and decades of memories.

Only one page remained unfinished. Just one.

The last page.

The last letter.

The Aakhri Khat.

Rishikesh adjusted his spectacles and picked up his pen.

Outside, he could hear faint laughter from the living room. Kehkasha was speaking on the phone. The sound made him smile.

His little girl.

The tiny child he had once carried through a midnight bus journey. The baby who had given him a reason to survive. The daughter who had unknowingly saved his life.

His eyes softened.

Then they drifted toward Aashna's photograph. A familiar ache settled inside his chest not painful anymore, just familiar. Like an old companion.

He opened the notebook, touched the blank page and began writing.

" *I wish you were mine in every lifetime, not stolen by destiny but borrowed by time*

I wish you were my wife

I wish we had raised kehkasha together, hand in hand, watching her grow, celebrating her victories, and worrying over her failures.

I wish I had grown old beside you, brushing silver strands from your hair, wrapping a shawl around your shoulders.

I wish you had called me your husband, your life partner, your home,

And I would have never stopped loving you. Not for a day, not for an hour, not even for a moment.

Destiny denied us a life together, but it never succeeded in teaching me how to stop loving you. Perhaps not in this lifetime, Aashna... but I will keep looking for you in every life that follows.

-Yours Forever

Rishikesh"

His pen stopped moving. The page was complete. For a moment, he simply stared at it.

Years.

Decades.

Memories.

Promises.

All of it had finally found its ending. A deep sense of peace settled over him, not happiness, not sadness. Just peace, the kind that arrives only when a journey is truly over.

Slowly, he leaned back into the chair. His gaze drifted toward Aashna's photograph one final time. A gentle smile appeared on his lips, a smile free from grief, free from longing, free from regret. Then, quietly, his eyes closed.

The pen slipped from his fingers and for the first time in decades, his tired heart rested.

Forever.

A few minutes later, Kehkasha entered the study carrying two cups of tea.

"Papa?"

No response.

She smiled. "You fell asleep again while writing, didn't you?"

She stepped closer. Then stopped, the smile faded in a span of second. The tea cups trembled in her hands.

"Papa?" Her voice shook.

The manuscript lay open before him. The final letter written and the final chapter finished.

And on his face remained the faintest smile. As though somewhere beyond this world, he had finally found the person he had spent a lifetime writing to.

Kehkasha lowered her head onto his shoulder and began to cry. But amidst the grief, her eyes landed on the last page. The final words her father had written for a woman he never stopped loving. Words that had travelled across decades, across pain, across destiny itself.

And there, at the bottom of the page, beneath the final sentence, stood his signature.

— Rishikesh

The room fell silent.

The letter was complete.

The story was complete.

Aakhri Khat had finally reached its destination.

Beyond This World

Rishikesh closed his eyes. The room faded, the manuscript faded, the years faded and the pain faded.

Finally, there was no ache in his chest. No memories clawing at his heart. No regrets weighing down his soul. There was only peace, a strange, comforting peace.

Then he heard a familiar voice. "Rishi..."

His breath caught. A voice he had carried within himself for a lifetime. Slowly, he turned. And there she was.

Aashna.

Standing a few steps away. The world around her looked unreal, washed in soft white light. Endless skies stretched in every direction. Birds drifted freely through the air. A gentle breeze moved through the silence, carrying a feeling of freedom he had never known before.

But he barely noticed any of it because all he could see was her.

Not the tired Aashna he had met in Bhaderwah, not the frightened bride hidden behind tears and jewellery, not the lifeless girl he had watched being taken away for her final journey.

This was his Aashna. The Aashna from the rainy afternoon, the girl in the purple kurti. Her hair open, wind playing with the loose strands, just as it always had. The same eyes, the same smile, the same girl he had fallen in love with all those years ago.

For a moment he simply stared.

Afraid.

Afraid that if he blinked, she would disappear again, afraid that destiny would once more steal her away.

Aashna smiled.

The kind of smile that had once made him believe in miracles.

Then she tilted her head slightly and asked, "Is baar itni der kyun laga di?"

His eyes immediately filled with tears. A laugh escaped him through the emotion.

"Raasta bahut lamba tha, Aashna."

Aashna's smile softened. She slowly extended her hand towards him

"Ab kahin nahi jaana."

Rishikesh looked at her hand. For years he had dreamed of this moment. For years he had searched for her in memories, in letters, in books, and in prayers he never believed in.

And now she was here.

Waiting.

Just as she always had.

Slowly, he reached forward and took her hand. For the first time in decades, he held her without fear, without fear of losing her, without fear of goodbyes, without fear of destiny.

Aashna intertwined her fingers with his. The way she should have done long ago.

Then together, they began to walk, no hurried steps, no separation waiting ahead, no unfinished letters, no missed timings. Just two souls moving forward side by side.

As they disappeared into the endless light, Rishikesh finally understood something destiny had taken a lifetime to teach him.

Some love stories do not end with a wedding, or end with growing old together.. Some are simply written across lifetimes.

And perhaps that was enough.

After all, destiny had separated them once.

Eternity did not.

Acknowledgement

First and foremost, To my father, **Mr Rajkumar** and my mother, **Mrs Chhaya.** Thank you for your endless love, support and motivation. Every achievement of mine is built upon the foundation you have provided.

A special thanks to my sisters, **Mrs Yashasvi** and **Mrs Nandini.** Your constant encouragement and faith in my abilities have always inspired me to pursue my dreams fearlessly.

I would like to thank **Mahak,** one of my very first readers. Thank you for reading my work with patience, encouraging me when I doubted myself, your excitement and belief in this story gave me the confidence to continue whenever I felt like giving up.

To **Jiya,** thank you for being one of the first people to read this story when it was just an idea finding its way onto paper.

To my little cousin **Katyayini,** thank you for admiring my words long before I called myself a writer. Your belief in my writing has been one of the purest forms of encouragement.

Lastly, thank you to everyone who has supported me, inspired me, and been a part of this journey in ways big and small. This book would not have been possible without you,

With gratitude and love

-Divyani Gupta

About The Author

Divyani Gupta is a nineteen-year-old writer, storyteller, and an avid reader who believes that some stories stay with us long after we turn the last page.

Aakhiri Khat is her debut novel—a tragic romance woven with love, longing, and the belief that some souls are destined to find each other, even if not in this lifetime.

When she isn't writing, Divyani enjoys reading novels, composing poetry, and imagining stories that explore the depths of human emotions. Through her writing, she hopes to create characters who feel real and stories that readers carry in their hearts.

Aakhiri Khat marks the beginning of her journey as an author, and she is grateful to every reader who chooses to be a part of it.

www.ingramcontent.com/pod-product-compliance
Lightning Source LLC
LaVergne TN
LVHW100317210926
848480LV00003B/1154